IMAGES ACROSS THE AGES

SOUTH AMERICAN PORTRAITS

Dorothy
and
Thomas Hoobler

Illustrations by
Stephen Marchesi

RAINTREE
STECK-VAUGHN
PUBLISHERS
The Steck-Vaughn Company

Austin, Texas

Copyright © 1994 Steck-Vaughn Company

All rights reserved. No part of this book may be reproduced or utilized in any form or by any means, electronic or mechanical, including photocopying, recording, or by any information storage and retrieval system, without permission in writing from the Publisher. Inquiries should be addressed to Steck-Vaughn, P.O. Box 26015, Austin, TX 78755.

Cover and interior design: Suzanne Beck
Electronic Production: Scott Melcer
Project Manager: Joyce Spicer

Library of Congress Cataloging-in-Publication Data
Hoobler, Dorothy.
    South American portraits / by Dorothy and Thomas Hoobler : illustrated by Stephen Marchesi.
      p.   cm. — (Images across the ages)
    Includes bibliographical references and index.
    ISBN 0-8114-6383-4
    1. South America — Biography — Juvenile literature. [1. South America — Biography.] I. Hoobler, Thomas. II. Marchesi, Stephen, ill. III. Title. IV. Series: Hoobler, Dorothy. Images across the ages
CT640.H66   1994
920.08—dc20   93-38361
                                                                       CIP AC

Printed and bound in the United States by Lake Book, Melrose Park, IL
1 2 3 4 5 6 7 8 9 0 LB 98 97 96 95 94 93

Acknowledgments
Excerpt from *One Hundred Years of Solitude* by Gabriel Garcia Marquez. English translation copyright © 1970 by Harper & Row Publishers, Inc. Reprinted by permission of HarperCollins Publishers, Inc.

CONTENTS

Introduction: El Dorado 4
1 "El Inca"—Garcilaso de la Vega 7
2 "The Little Rose"—Rose of Lima 14
3 The Little Cripple—
   Antônio Francisco Lisboa 20
4 The Liberators—Simón Bolívar and
   José de San Martín 26
5 A Tough Survivor—Maria Antônio Muniz 35
6 School Teacher to a Nation—Domingo
   Faustino Sarmiento 42
7 The Tin King—Simón I. Patiño 49
8 A Passionate Voice—Gabriela Mistral 56
9 The Song of Brazil—Heitor Villa-Lobos 63
10 "I Will Be Somebody"—Evita Perón 69
11 "The Black Pearl"—Pelé 76
12 "Daily Miracles"—Gabriel García Márquez 83
Glossary 90
Bibliography 91
Sources 93
Index 95

INTRODUCTION

El Dorado

In February 1541, an immense group of men and animals assembled in the main square of Quito, an ancient city in what is today's South American country of Ecuador. Some of the men rode horses and wore shiny metal breastplates and helmets. These were Spanish *conquistadors*, or conquerors, who had appeared off the coast of Ecuador just 15 years before. In that brief span of time, the Spanish, led by Francisco Pizarro, had conquered the vast Inca Empire that stretched far down the west coast of South America. Now, Francisco Pizarro's brother Gonzalo prepared to lead an expedition over the Andes Mountains to explore the interior of the continent.

The goals of the conquistadors were "God, gold, and glory"— with emphasis on gold. Nothing inspired the conquistadors more than the tale of El Dorado, "the Gilded Man," a ruler so wealthy that his body was said to be covered with gold powder. Just two years earlier, the conquistador Jiménez de Quesada had landed on the northern coast of South America and slogged through mountains and jungles in search of the kingdom of El Dorado.

Gonzalo Pizarro was about to chase after another dream. He had heard that a great stand of precious cinnamon trees grew somewhere to the east. On February 21, he set out with 350 conquistadors on what would be one of the most heroic journeys ever made. He prepared for a long trip. The expedition included 4,000 "volunteers"—Native Americans who had been enslaved by the Spanish after the downfall of the Inca Empire. They led 2,000 llamas burdened with provisions and weapons. For good measure, Gonzalo brought along 2,000 ferocious dogs to frighten any Native Americans they might meet, and another 2,000 hogs to be used as food.

However, the journey up the western slopes of the Andes Mountains was more difficult than Pizarro expected. Fierce, icy winds and blizzards took a terrible toll. In the thin air 20,000 feet above sea level, men and animals dropped from exhaustion. The survivors descended into the jungle on the other side, where the climate was radically different. The conquistadors had entered what others would call the "Green Hell"—the enormous rain forest along the equator. In the constant rainfall and oppressive heat, the conquistadors' armor rusted and disintegrated. Pizarro's band hacked its way through the forest for eight months.

At last they reached the banks of the Napo River. A few cinnamon trees, hardly a treasure, were all that the expedition had found. Most of their animals had been eaten, even the dogs, and the explorers faced starvation. At a spot which today bears the name El Barco, "the boat," Pizarro made a decision. They would build a boat to send a group downriver to look for food.

Pizarro selected his cousin, a one-eyed knight named Francisco de Orellana, to lead the search party. But as time went on and the food gave out entirely, Pizarro decided Orellana must be dead. Surviving by eating roots and the leather of their own boots, Pizarro and his remaining men struggled back to Quito.

Meanwhile, Orellana and his 57 men had found that the river's current was so swift that they could not turn around. Each day they were swept helplessly ever farther into an unknown and hostile region. Gaspar de Carvajal, a Spanish friar who accompanied Orellana's group, related that they were certain that death was near: "I said Mass, as it is said at sea, commending to Our Lord our persons and our lives, beseeching Him...to deliver us from such manifest hardship and destruction—for that is what it was coming to look like to us now."

Orellana and his men had entered the headwaters of the mightiest river on earth. The Incas called it *Amaru-Mayu*—"great serpent-mother of men." The Spanish were saved from starvation when one of the tribes who lived along the river gave them food. But the native people warned Orellana that farther downriver was a kingdom ruled by fierce women. The story reminded the Spaniards of the Amazons, women warriors of Greek mythology.

Now the tales appeared to come true. On one of the bends of the river, as the Spaniards approached a village, a shower of arrows suddenly came at them. The Spanish fired back with their harquebuses, or muskets. Friar de Carvajal described the encounter:

> In spite of all the harm we were doing them, some of them kept on fighting and others dancing....I wish to tell the reason these Indians defended themselves so stoutly. It should be known that they are vassals and tributaries of the Amazons, and...as many as ten of those women came, and we saw them leading all those Indians in the fighting like captains, and they fought so boldly that the Indians did not dare fall back...if one of [the Indians] attempted to retreat... [the Amazons] killed him with the blows of their clubs, and this is the reason why the Indians defended themselves so bravely. These women are very white and tall, and have very long hair which they wear braided and wrapped around their head, and they are very strong.

No one else ever saw these Amazons. Some modern scholars think that they might have been Tapuya women, who customarily fought side by side with the men. Orellana's group, with so many arrows sticking out of the sides of their boat that it looked "like a porcupine," escaped to tell the tale. The episode gave this mighty river its name—the Amazon.

Many months later, after a journey of 3,000 miles down the river, Orellana reached the Atlantic Ocean. The date was August 26, 1542. Ironically, Orellana and his men were unaware that a Portuguese settlement lay nearby. Just as Portugal and Spain share the Iberian Peninsula in Europe, colonists from the two nations would share South America in the New World. Orellana and his men sailed north, reaching a Spanish-settled island off Venezuela.

Even today, Orellana's epic trip would be difficult to duplicate. His voyage down the Amazon left the Spanish in awe of the continent they had claimed. One conquistador declared that the continent held "many great and strange things." He was not exaggerating. The continent's mighty rivers, mountains, deserts, jungles, and vast grasslands are on a grand scale, dwarfing Spain itself, which is only about 5 percent of the size of what were once its South American colonies. Portugal, Spain's neighbor on the Iberian Peninsula, also claimed territory in the New World—Brazil. Today Brazil is the largest nation in South America and nearly 100 times as large as Portugal.

The stories of the people who made history here also have an outsized quality. Men and women of all races, they have always pursued great dreams, searching for the new and marvelous and magical.

CHAPTER 1

"El Inca"—Garcilaso de la Vega

In April 1548, the streets of Cuzco, Peru, buzzed with the news that Gonzalo Pizarro had been sentenced to death. A 9-year-old boy, Garcilaso de la Vega, later recalled, "We left school early to go and watch the execution." Little Garcilaso witnessed the punishment with sadness, for his father was a friend of Gonzalo's. Often Garcilaso and Gonzalo's son had run races under the eyes of the old conquistador himself.

Gonzalo Pizarro, who once had shod his horses with gold and silver shoes, had finally aimed too high. Though the conquistador had triumphed in battles where he was outnumbered by 200 to one and had survived the trip over the Andes, he had overestimated his own power. After returning to Quito with 80 survivors of the disastrous expedition, Gonzalo learned that his brother Francisco had been assassinated in his palace in Lima. The king of Spain had sent his own representative, called a *viceroy*, to take control of the lands that the conquistadors had won. In response, Gonzalo declared himself ruler of the rich kingdom of Peru.

The royal viceroy, however, had more than enough soldiers to shatter Gonzalo's dream. The conquistador was beheaded and his followers were publicly whipped. It was an important moment in the history of the Spanish empire of South America, for it marked the end of the conquistador era and the beginning of rule by the Spanish crown.

Garcilaso, the little boy who watched the executioner hold up Gonzalo's severed head before the crowd, would one day write the history of these troubled times. He had a special point of view, for he was a *mestizo*—the child of a Spanish father and an Inca mother, thus combining both the conqueror and the conquered.

Twenty years before Garcilaso's birth, his mother's and father's people did not even know each other existed. Rumors about a rich empire to the south reached the Spaniards who had settled in Panama, the slender strip of land connecting South America to North America. Francisco Pizarro, who had been a swineherder in Spain, dreamed of gold and glory and hoped to duplicate the feat of Hernan Cortés, who had conquered the Aztec Empire of Mexico. Setting out from Panama with three ships in 1528, Pizarro landed on the coast of Peru.

Stretching along the west coast of the continent from Colombia to Chile was an empire ruled by the Incas, heirs to a great civilization that had existed in the Andes for over 1,500 years. These people called their kingdom Tawantinsuyu—"Land of the Four Quarters"—and made their capital at Cuzco, "the navel of the world." The Inca rulers (who were called "the Inca") claimed to be the descendants of the sun. The Incas developed a code of laws to govern the empire and unified it by building roads over some of the most rugged terrain on earth. Trained runners raced along the roads in relays from one station to the next, bringing orders to all corners of the Inca Empire. Huge granaries stored food, such as beans, chile peppers, and potatoes, for times of famine.

Francisco Pizarro had luck on his side, for at the time he arrived, the Inca Empire was split by fighting. When the old ruler, Huayna Capac, died, two of his sons fought to become his successor. Atahualpa was the son who won the title of Inca, but the war left the empire in a weakened state.

Hearing that the Spaniards were marching toward his capital, Atahualpa offered to meet Pizarro at Cayamarca, in today's Peru. Arriving first, Pizarro prepared an ambush. When Atahualpa arrived with an enormous retinue of followers in August 1532, the Spaniards' guns mowed down the Inca's forces. The Inca people would remember this as the day when "night fell at noon." According to Garcilaso de la Vega's history:

> The Spanish cavalrymen left their hiding places, hurling themselves like thunderbolts at the Indian squadrons....Don Pizarro and his wildly impatient infantrymen had succeeded, meanwhile, in forcing their way to Atahualpa, because at the very idea of so rich a catch they already saw themselves the masters of all the treasures in Peru. The Indians crowded about the royal litter, ready to defend with their own bodies the Inca's sacred person. They were massacred one by one.

After falling into Pizarro's hands, Atahualpa offered a great treasure in return for his freedom. From throughout the empire, the Inca's people brought the ransom to Pizarro and his followers. Dazzled by wealth beyond their wildest dreams, the Spaniards eagerly scooped up their loot, but treacherously killed Atahualpa anyway. Pizarro's soldiers then fanned out through the Inca Empire, conquering Cuzco and other important cities. Without a ruler, the Incas were defeated little by little. By 1536, the Spaniards had subdued most of the remaining opposition.

Among the companions of Francisco Pizarro was Sebastian Garcilaso de la Vega, a Spaniard of distinguished background. While in Cuzco, Sebastian fell in love with the Inca princess Nusta Chimpu Ocllo. She was a member of the Inca *acllausi*, or "house of the chosen women," where women of the royal family lived.

After being baptized in the Roman Catholic faith, Nusta took the name Isabel. On April 12, 1539, she gave birth to Sebastian's son, Garcilaso. Although Sebastian never married Isabel, he attended her child's baptism, a sign that he recognized their relationship, and he took both Isabel and the boy into his home.

Young Garcilaso grew up in Cuzco during dangerous times, for fighting now broke out among the conquistadors. After Francisco Pizarro's assassination by rival Spaniards, Pizarro's four brothers battled to keep control of his empire in Peru. At one point, when the fighting reached Cuzco, Isabel and her young son had to escape from Sebastian's house over the rooftops in the dead of night. When the Spanish king sent his viceroy to exert control, Sebastian de la Vega turned his back on the Pizarros, shrewdly changing sides to save his neck.

Even at an early age, Sebastian's young son had a sense that his destiny was tied to both the peoples whose blood flowed in his veins. Garcilaso received a traditional Spanish education in Latin, religion, and history. In addition, he learned horsemanship and the fighting skills necessary for any Spanish gentleman. Though a mestizo, the boy was welcome in the homes of his father's Spanish friends.

However, when his father married a Spanish woman, she was uncomfortable with this reminder of her husband's earlier love. Garcilaso and his mother moved into a separate house, where she and her relatives taught him about his Inca heritage and how to

speak Quechua, the Inca language. He later recalled those times:

> Every week, the members of [my mother's] family...came to visit her. On these occasions, the conversation turned almost invariably to the origin of our kings and to their majesty....Then leaving grandeur behind, my relatives would turn to the present, and here they wept over their dead kings and their lost empire. Indeed, I do not believe that there was a single one of these conversations that did not end in tears and wailing, while all those present kept repeating: "Once we were kings, now we are vassals!" Being but a child, I came and went freely amongst them, and I listened to what they said with the rapt attention with which, at this age, one listens to fairy tales.

This was how the young mestizo learned the Inca history that he would later write. His oldest relative, an uncle, told him the origin of his people:

> You should know that in the old days the whole of this region was covered in scrub and heath, and the people lived like wild beasts, with no religion or government, not towns or houses, without sowing the soil and without clothing.... Our Father the Sun, seeing men in this state, took pity on them, and sent from Heaven a Son and a Daughter to teach them about Himself and persuade them to adopt Him as their God and worship

Him...and learn to till the soil and grow plants and crops and breed flocks and use the fruits of the earth like rational beings and not like beasts. With these instructions our Father the Sun set His two children down beside Lake Titicaca [the huge lake that borders Peru and Bolivia], and bade them to go forth.

As Garcilaso related the story, the Sun told his children that wherever they stopped to sleep, they should try to plunge a golden rod into the ground. The place where it sank would be their kingdom, where they would be "lords and kings over all people."

Traveling north from Lake Titicaca, the divine brother and sister tried to push the golden rod into the earth, but the earth would not yield. Finally, they came to the valley of Cuzco, where the golden rod sank and disappeared. Now the sister and brother called together all the people in the valley and told them that they had been sent to teach them new skills. The people, attracted by the couple's elaborate clothes and gold jewelry, listened and obeyed. Under the couple's direction, they built the city of Cuzco. The brother taught the men to till and plant the land and to bring water down the mountainside in ditches. His sister taught the women the skills of weaving and spinning.

Young Garcilaso loved the stories of how the descendants of the divine couple, the Incas, conquered an ever-greater empire. When the boy reached manhood, he took the name Garcilaso de la Vega, El Inca, reflecting both sides of his heritage. Garcilaso was in a unique position to see the roots of both cultures. As much as he loved the Inca heritage, he became a devout Christian. He held equal respect for both his father's and his mother's cultures. When his father died in 1559, Garcilaso claimed the right to inherit his property, but was refused. The next year he decided to argue his case before the Spanish king's court in Madrid.

Before leaving Cuzco, he took a trip to the old Inca palace to visit his mother's ancestors. He was able to see them almost as they were in life, for the Incas successfully mummified the bodies of their rulers. Garcilaso stared into their ancient faces. He later recalled, "All of these bodies were so well preserved that not a hair, not an eyebrow, not an eyelash was missing. I remember touching one finger of Huayna Capac's hand: it was hard as wood." In his writings, he would bring these kings to life again.

As Garcilaso left Cuzco on the solid stone road built by the

Incas, the clinking of the mule's hooves drummed in his ears. He did not know that he would never return.

In Spain, some of his father's relatives helped him gain an audience with the Spanish king. The king refused to grant Garcilaso his father's estates, but offered to make him an officer in the Spanish Army. Garcilaso accepted. His training in Cuzco stood him in good stead as he served in Spanish wars in Italy and North Africa. After his commander died, Garcilaso retired. However, as he explained later:

> I came back from the war with such losses and such debts that it was impossible for me to ask for another audience at court, and I therefore preferred to withdraw into loneliness and poverty, in order to lead the calm and peaceful life of a disillusioned man who has taken leave of this fickle world and expects nothing more from it.

Garcilaso went to live at Cordoba in Spain, where he began to write. His first book was *The Florida of the Inca*, about the adventures of the conquistador Hernando de Soto in the southeastern part of today's United States. De Soto had also served with Pizarro.

As an old man, Garcilaso finally set down the story of his mother's people in *The Royal Commentaries of the Incas*. By this time, he had entered a religious order and he dedicated the work to "Our Lady, the Very Immaculate Virgin Mary, Mother of God." Now he relived his youth in Cuzco, recalling all the lore he had heard from those who had lived during the great age of the Inca. He died peacefully in 1616 and was buried in a chapel of the great cathedral of Cordoba.

Garcilaso de la Vega, "El Inca," was the first important Spanish-American writer. His prose is still treasured throughout the Spanish-speaking world. He believed that his life's mission was to teach the world about the Inca civilization. As an old man he said, "I have no reason to regret that fortune has not always smiled on me, since I am indebted to this fact for the opening up of my literary career which, I believe, will give me wider and more lasting fame than might be expected from any sort of material success." History has proved that he was right.

CHAPTER 2

"The Little Rose"—Rose of Lima

On a spring day in 1586, in the city of Lima, Peru, a servant of the Flores family looked in on the newborn infant Isabelita. As she watched the baby sleeping in her crib, her eyes widened in amazement. On the infant's cheeks, two beautiful roses were forming. The servant excitedly called relatives and neighbors to see the wondrous sight of the roses blooming on Isabelita's face. They too saw the roses, and believed they must be a sign of God's special favor on the child.

Roses were important in Christianity as the symbol of purity and sacrifice. To the devout, the Virgin Mary was popularly known as "the rose without thorns." In paintings Mary was pictured decked with roses. Just 13 years earlier, Miguel Acosta had planted the first rose bush in Lima, in the garden of the Espiritu Santo hospital just behind the Flores house. When the first roses bloomed, so great was the enthusiasm of the Limeños (inhabitants of Lima) that they carried a huge bouquet to the great cathedral and laid it at the feet of the Virgin.

"She is a Rose," exclaimed the Flores family's servant, and the name stuck, even though the baby had been baptized Isabel. The roses faded as she grew up, but friends and neighbors pointed out "the Little Rose," recalling the miraculous sign. Rose's life would exceed their expectations.

Rose was born in April 1586 into a family of eight children. Her father, Gaspar de Flores, held a minor position in the militia of Lima. The Flores family lived in modest circumstances in a small house by the Rímac River. Rose's mother, Maria de Olivia, worked all her life as a seamstress to make ends meet and supplement her husband's earnings. Young Rose herself took up the needle to help support the family.

Even as a child, Rose spent long hours in prayer. When neighboring children came to play with their dolls, Rose took no part. When asked why she did not join in the fun she replied, "Because they say that the Devil sometimes talks through the mouth of dolls." Indeed, the idols that were still worshiped by the native people looked like dolls. So strong was Rose's fear of sinning that she would hide in dark parts of the house to be alone.

Rose's behavior caused the other children to laugh at her. Her mother Maria wanted her daughter to grow up normally, but realized that there was something special about this child. Once, when Rose became very ill with a high fever, her mother feared she was going to die. She asked a servant to go buy a chocolate drink to strengthen her. But Rose called her back, saying that the chocolate was already on its way. Within a short time, the door opened and a servant from a nearby house appeared with a gift—a large silver cup filled with chocolate. When her mother asked Rose how she knew it was coming, Rose smiled and said she had sent her guardian angel for it.

Despite Rose's religious leanings, her mother hoped that Rose would one day marry and have a family. But Rose was determined to become a *beata*, a woman who devoted her life to the Church without formally joining a community of nuns. Beatas wore a religious garment, did not marry, and practiced religious devotions and acts of charity. Many people regarded the beatas as specially blessed by God, endowed with almost supernatural powers. In the deeply religious society of Lima, the beatas commanded great prestige. Both rich and poor often brought gifts and asked the beatas to intercede on their behalf with God.

As Rose's love of solitude grew, she asked her brother Fernando to build a shrine where she could go to pray. He set to work on a little hut with an altar that he covered with pictures of the saints and the Madonna. Banana fronds, over a yard long, enclosed the structure to give privacy. Each day after completing her sewing duties, Rose fled to this little place of refuge overlooking the family garden. In solitude, she prayed and sometimes even whipped herself with a belt or chain to atone for her sinful ways.

Lima, with its hot, humid climate, was a breeding ground for ferocious mosquitoes. Yet visitors noticed that although hordes of the insects swarmed over Rose's hut, she was never bitten. Rose explained,

When I moved into this house the mosquitoes and I made a friendly agreement: I would not bother them or drive them away and they not bite me or make a noise; and we live in such friendship that they neither bite nor annoy me; on the contrary, they help me to praise the Lord with the hum of their buzzing.

Other signs of divine blessing appeared. People saw that the flowers in the garden outside Rose's hut bloomed out of season. She could sometimes be heard singing in a beautiful voice and playing the guitar. So clear and pure was her music that it attracted the birds, who came to sing with her. "Come, little nightingale," Rose would sing, "Let us praise the Lord. Raise a song to your Creator, I shall sing unto my Savior."

Rose's refuge was not always peaceful, for during her long hours of prayer, the devil sometimes came to tempt and disturb her. One night the devil hid in a basket, making such a terrible noise that she could not pray. Making the sign of the cross over herself, Rose blew out the candle and challenged the devil to a fight. He suddenly appeared in the form of a giant. Grabbing her by the shoulders, he shook her until she thought her bones would shatter. But reminding herself that God protected her, she laughed and told the devil he was too weak to defeat her faith.

Rose sometimes left her solitude to take part in the religious processions that celebrated the many feast days of the Catholic Church calendar. However, she always tried to avoid the *tapadas* who promenaded boldly through the streets of Lima. The tapadas stood in stark contrast to the beatas. They were worldly women who dressed in the latest fashion—gowns short enough to show off their tiny feet shod in velvet slippers. The hallmark of the tapada was a long shawl which she tightly wrapped around herself to show off the contours of her body. The shawl also covered her face—though only one eye was allowed to peep out, the tapada handled her shawl with the same skill as the bullfighter used a cape. With an alluring gesture and the wink of her bright eye, she could attract the ardor of the men of the city, both married and unmarried.

The city officials disapproved of the tapadas, but the women used their shawls not only to attract men but to hide their identities. The word *tapar* means "to hide" and in this disguise, women flirted in a way that they would not do with their faces bare. A woman from a respectable family could leave her home with her head uncovered. Then when she got far enough away she would wrap the shawl around herself and act as she pleased. The story is told of one tapada who flirted with her own husband at a party. When he responded to her advances, she tore off her shawl and accused him of unfaithfulness. Throughout the colonial history of Lima, foreign visitors always commented on the amazing boldness of the tapadas.

Rose also served as a *camerera* for the churches of Lima. A camerera was the person who was permitted to go behind the altar to dress the statue of the Virgin Mary and put on its crown and jewels before it was brought out for processions. The camerera had great prestige, for people regarded her work as more than simply playing with a doll. It was thought that this honor gave her such an intimate relationship with the Virgin, that she could ask Christ's mother to answer people's prayers.

Over the years, Rose's fame grew. She was spoken of as the savior of the city, the person who atoned for the many sins of the Limeños and the tapadas. People from all levels of society visited her secluded shrine. Wealthy people brought gifts of money, clothing, and food, which Rose distributed to the poor. Some came to ask Rose to teach them how to sew, for her beautiful embroidery was said to be the finest in Peru. She also taught music and poetry in addition to Catholic wisdom.

When Rose was 31, a story spread through Lima that she was responsible for a miracle. At this time, Rose had accepted the invitation of a wealthy, charitable woman to stay at her home. The woman proudly unveiled a painting of Christ that she had placed in her private chapel. As Rose knelt before the painting, beads of perspiration appeared on the face of Christ. The members of the household rushed to see the miracle, and cried out with joy and amazement. Only Rose remained calm and serene.

The artist who had painted the picture came to examine it. Skeptically, he thought that something must have caused his paints to run. But he discovered that the perspiration only appeared on the face, and nowhere else. There seemed to be no natural explanation. The story of the miraculous painting convinced many others that Rose was a living saint.

Four months later, on August 24, 1617, Rose died in a room off the chapel with the miraculous painting. Even though the hour was late, word of her death immediately spread all over Lima. The city went into a turmoil of grief. Thousands of people surrounded the house, weeping and praying in a nightlong vigil. The next day, as Rose's body was carried through the streets, crowds rushed forward to touch it. The viceroy himself paid his respects in front of the viceregal palace on the main square of Lima. Most of Lima turned out for her funeral.

Popular devotion to Rose continued after her death and many miracles were attributed to her. In 1671, she was canonized by the Roman Catholic Church, becoming the first American saint.

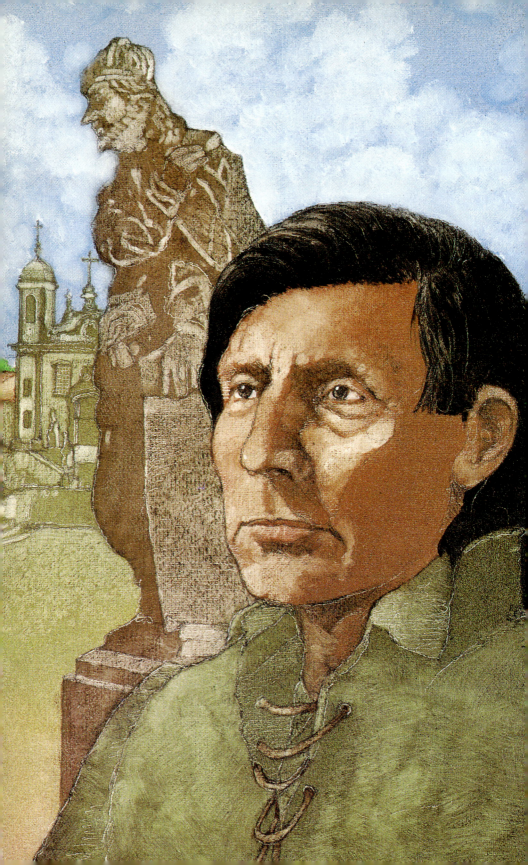

CHAPTER 3

THE LITTLE CRIPPLE—
ANTÔNIO FRANCISCO LISBOA

In the late 1770's, a middle-aged man named Antônio Francisco Lisboa sat in his studio in Ouro Prêto, Brazil. His dark skin and curved nose marked him as a *pardo*, or man of mixed race. Around him were drawing boards, chisels, and mallets, the tools of his trade. An architect and sculptor, Lisboa had created many of the beautiful churches in this gold-mining boom town.

Lisboa was worried. Recently, he had experienced disturbing and mysterious physical changes. Strange growths and lumps swelled on his fingers. His hands seemed to be losing their ability to move and feel. These were the first signs of leprosy, a disease that would eventually cause him the loss of his hands and feet and turn his face into a grotesque mask. The future seemed terrifying to a man whose whole life was devoted to working with his hands.

Yet Antônio Lisboa would persevere, for he was a man of heroic will. In the second half of his life, against enormous odds, Antônio would create his greatest masterpieces. Because of his affliction, contemporaries called him *O Aleijadinho*, Portuguese for "The Little Cripple." Under that name he would become known as the greatest sculptor of colonial South America.

Antônio was born on the outskirts of Ouro Prêto in 1738, the illegitimate son of a Portuguese gentleman and an African slave. His father, Manuel Francisco de Lisboa, was one of the many Portuguese who had come to the colony of Brazil to seek their fortunes. From the year 1500, when Portuguese sailors first sighted its coastline, Brazil's riches had attracted adventurers.

The colony experienced continuous cycles of "boom and bust." Its original attraction had been the brazilwood trees along the coast that had given the colony its name. They provided a red dye that was highly prized in Europe, but the Portuguese were more interested in the spice trade with the Indies on the other side of the world. To encourage colonization, the Portuguese government introduced sugarcane plantations in the far northeast of today's Brazil. African slaves were brought to work the sugar fields.

The first Portuguese settlements hugged the shoreline of the Atlantic, but the lure of gold enticed explorers into the dense jungles of the interior. These ambitious adventurers, known as *bandeirantes*, or "flag-bearers," pushed Portugal's New World domain ever farther to the west. Finally, in 1693, gold was discovered and the greatest gold rush in the Americas up to this time was on. Hordes of people poured into the area, which was called Minas Gerais, or "General Mines." Among them was Antônio's father.

Manuel settled near Ouro Prêto, a boom town that had already grown to more than 60,000 people, making it then the largest city in Brazil. The city was named Ouro Prêto ("Black Gold") because the gold ore of the region turned black when it was exposed to the air. Newly rich prospectors built mansions along the narrow, crooked streets of Ouro Prêto's steep hills. To glorify their city, they sponsored the construction of beautiful churches. Manuel, a carpenter, soon found that his old trade could make him more money than searching for gold. He earned the rank of master builder and became involved in the design and planning of the churches.

Because Manuel's child Antônio had an African mother, the boy was born a slave, but his father granted him freedom at his baptism. After his father married a Portuguese woman, Antônio moved into their household.

Growing up, Antônio visited the construction sites where his father worked, soaking up the knowledge of sculpting and architecture. He played at chipping stone and timber with young clumsy hands. Somehow he also learned to read and write and at a young age began his apprenticeship in his father's workshop.

A new church dedicated to St. Francis of Assisi marked the start of Antônio's artistic career. He would continue work on it throughout most of his lifetime, carving ornate decorations on the outer walls of the building and making statues for the interior as well. He discovered that he could work best with soapstone, a soft, bluish mineral that was found throughout Minas Gerais. Other sculptors had ignored it, favoring harder materials, such as granite and marble, but Antônio shaped it so beautifully that soapstone statues by other artists soon appeared in churches all over the region. Even today, however, art scholars can tell at a glance which ones are Antônio's.

Antônio's art was strongly influenced by the European style known as Baroque, brought to Brazil by Jesuit missionaries. The Baroque style, with its rich, elaborate decoration, was meant to inspire worshipers with the grandeur of God. Working closely with the priests in building churches, Antônio developed a deep religious feeling, and all of his works have sacred themes. He eagerly read the Scriptures, a practice that would bring him comfort in later life. Woodcuts and prints in the Bibles and religious books from Europe frequently inspired him. Indeed, these illustrations helped him to design his statues and accurately carve animals, such as lambs, which he had never actually seen.

In the first years of his success, Antônio was known as a man filled with the love of life. Handsome and charming, he attracted young women wherever he went. Commissions for his work poured in from all the neighboring towns, and Antônio prospered.

Everything changed when his leprosy appeared. Over time his limbs became totally deformed and he lost his toes and fingers. Always in pain, he was finally reduced to hobbling around on his knees. The skin of his face began to flake off in ugly sores. Fearing that people viewed him with fear and loathing, he began to work only behind a screen so no one could see him. He started early in the morning and did not leave till late at night, hoping that the

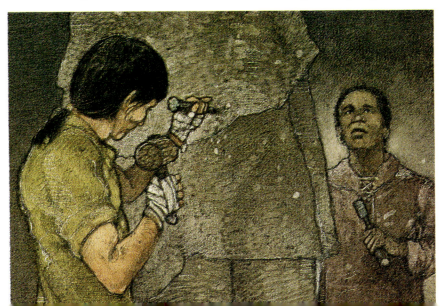

darkness would hide his ugliness. The once lively and cheerful sculptor gradually cut himself off from human contact. Only his own three slaves were allowed to come near him. Sometimes, when his depression became too great, Antônio tried to harm himself with his chisels, and the slaves had to take them away.

Mauricio, who was both Antônio's slave and his closest friend, now became his assistant as well. Mauricio fitted leather pads to his master's knees so that he could move about and climb the high ladders that he had to use. Antônio taught Mauricio all he knew about sculpting so that the slave could do some of the work. But Antônio's great genius could not be taught, and Mauricio gently closed his master's crippled hands around the hammer and chisel so that he could make the stone come to life.

In 1789, an independence movement arose in the Minas Gerais region, aiming to free Brazil from Portuguese rule. The king of Portugal had always collected his *quinto,* or one-fifth of all the wealth that came from the mines. In addition to this, the Portuguese government levied high taxes, which caused hardship and resentment. One of the leaders of the freedom movement was a dentist, Joaquim Jose da Silva Xavier. The miners called him Tiradentes, or "the tooth-puller." He had corresponded with Thomas Jefferson and was inspired by the United States Declaration of Independence. Idealistically, Tiradentes advocated the end of slavery in addition to independence. But government troops discovered the plans for revolt and arrested the leaders. Although most of them were only exiled, Tiradentes was tortured and beheaded. His head was set up in the main square of Ouro Prêto as a warning. Although he failed, the anniversary of Tiradentes's execution is today a national holiday in Brazil.

In the turmoil of this time, Antônio Lisboa found work in an isolated place called Congonhas do Campo. Here, though crippled and tormented by doubts, he would create his greatest masterpiece. At this spot, high in the mountains of Minas Gerais province, a church had been built to celebrate a miracle. An unsuccessful gold miner had developed a fatal illness and prayed to God to cure it. When he recovered, he raised a cross on the spot where he had prayed, and devoted his life to building a great church there. Walking from town to town as a beggar, he raised only enough for a small shrine. After his death, however, many pilgrims traveled to the shrine and contributed more money for the dead man's dream. When the building was finally raised, it was decided that only Antônio Lisboa, the crippled sculptor, could decorate it.

Perhaps attracted by the story of a miraculous cure, Antônio accepted. People doubted that he could do the job. One who saw him said he was "so sickly that he has to be carried everywhere and has to have his chisels strapped to him to be able to work."

Knowing this would be his last major project, Antônio pulled together all his resources and created one of the marvels of world art at the Church of Bom Jesus de Matosinhos. Directing teams of stonecutters, carpenters, and wood-carvers, he organized the huge project, which would take him nine years to complete. Six small chapels in a garden leading to the main church contain scenes from the passion of Christ. They are filled with 65 cedarwood figures of Christ, the apostles, Roman soldiers, and Mary Magdalene. Each is wonderfully lifelike; visitors today can see the veins of Christ's neck and his individual muscles. As a soldier blows a trumpet, his cheeks bulge grotesquely. The Christ figures are often presented with a red mark around the neck, which many believe means that they also represent the rebel Tiradentes. The Roman soldiers in the scenes wear Portuguese boots and Antônio carved them with two left feet and vicious faces.

During the construction of this first part of the project, Antônio's friend, the African slave Mauricio, died. The crippled sculptor struggled on despite his loss. His final plan was to place 12 soapstone statues of the Hebrew prophets alongside the steps leading up to the church. Larger than life-size, the statues guard the entrance sternly, with their arms upraised and their bodies twisted in warning. Their appearance reminds the onlooker of Antônio's torture. It is almost as if he enlarged his art, giving his work the physical power that he himself had lost. Each blow of the chisel must have cost him unbearable pain. With the completion of this work in 1805, Antônio Lisboa finished his artistic career.

For the rest of his life, Antônio adopted a hermit's existence, refusing to see anyone except his daughter-in-law. Lying helpless on a bed of bare boards, he complained about the money that people owed him. His torments came to an end in 1814, when he was over 75. But his work survives, celebrating the great spirit of the man people called O Aleijadinho, "the little cripple."

CHAPTER 4

THE LIBERATORS—SIMÓN BOLÍVAR AND JOSÉ DE SAN MARTÍN

On July 26, 1822, Simón Bolívar stood on the dock at the Pacific port city of Guayaquil, in today's Ecuador. He was waiting for José de San Martín. The two men, the most famous figures in South American history, were about to meet for the first time. It was an important moment, for the Spanish colonies' war of independence had reached a crucial stage. By capturing Guayaquil, Bolívar had virtually completed the liberation of the northern part of the continent. Meanwhile, San Martín had been equally successful in the south. It was time to discuss what kind of government would replace the Spanish viceroys.

The two freedom fighters were a study in contrasts. Although they were both courageous men who let nothing stand in the way of their zeal for independence, they had very different personalities. Bolívar was dramatic and emotional in his every deed and gesture. He gloried in all the awards and decorations bestowed on him. San Martín, on the other hand, was a man of few words, who had no use for honors and gifts.

After greeting each other at the dock, they spoke in private for an hour. Then it was time for a grand banquet, attended by their staffs. Bolívar raised his glass in a toast: "To the two greatest men in South America—General San Martín and myself." To which San Martín replied, "To the early end of the war; to the organization of the republics of the continent and to the health of the Liberator of Colombia [Bolívar]."

The next day, the two met for four hours in secret discussions. No one knows what was said, but it was apparent that they had a serious disagreement.

Though each had fought for independence, they were at odds over the future of South America. San Martín favored a king with

limited powers, like the king of England. Bolívar was a strong republican. That night, during a ball held to celebrate victory, San Martín slipped away and left Guayaquil. The two great liberators never met again.

Simón Bolívar was born in Caracas, in today's Venezuela, on July 24, 1783, to a wealthy family. Caracas was then in the Viceroyalty of New Grenada, which included today's Colombia, Venezuela, and Ecuador. Both of Simón's parents died during his childhood and his education was in the hands of two tutors, Simón Rodríguez and Andres Bello. Rodríguez introduced the boy to his love of the great eighteenth-century French thinkers, whose ideas on freedom inspired both French and American revolutionaries. Bolívar acknowledged his tutor's strong influence years later in a letter. "You have molded my heart for liberty, justice, greatness and beauty. I have followed the path you traced for me."

At 17 Bolívar went to Spain to continue his education. His wealth made this young *criollo* (a person of Spanish ancestry born in America) welcome in court circles. Here he met and married Maria Teresa del Toro, but she died soon after they returned to Caracas. Grief-stricken, Bolívar vowed never to marry again. Instead he set off for France and a life of pleasure.

He was in Paris when Napoleon crowned himself emperor. Bolívar never forgot the grand pageantry of the occasion, and strove to match it in later years. In 1805 he visited Rome with his old tutor Rodríguez. The sight inspired the young man with thoughts of the great days when Rome had been a republic of free men. He fell on his knees and made a vow to God that he would not rest until his country was freed from the control of Spain.

Returning home, Bolívar began to work against Spanish rule. He soon found supporters among the other criollos, who resented the fact that they were treated as inferiors by the *peninsulares*— those who had been born in Spain. The top jobs in the colonial government were reserved for peninsulares, who made no secret of the fact that they looked on the criollos as their social inferiors.

In addition, the colonies were run for the benefit of Spain. The colonial government imposed high taxes on the people, and the money went back to Spain. Trade with the United States and Europe was strictly controlled, making it difficult for the colonists to find other markets for their products. These economic policies added to the criollos' discontent.

When the French ruler Napoleon invaded Spain in 1808, he captured the royal family and put his own brother on the throne. The Venezuelan criollos moved quickly to take advantage of the situation. Bolívar hurried to Great Britain to try and persuade its government to aid the cause of independence. When he returned home, he brought with him Francisco de Miranda, a Venezuelan patriot who had led an unsuccessful rebellion earlier. The 60-year-old Miranda was a respected figure, and the other criollos rallied around him. A colonial congress was called and on July 5, 1811, declared Venezuela independent from Spain.

Then a terrible disaster occurred. One of the worst earthquakes in the history of the Americas devastated Caracas and killed many of the patriots. When Spain sent an army to crush the independence movement, the weakened Venezuelans suffered an overwhelming defeat. Miranda was imprisoned and Bolívar went off to Colombia to enlist volunteer soldiers. Bringing his forces back to Venezuela in March 1813, he attacked the Spanish successfully. He marched triumphantly into Caracas in August. Hailed by his compatriots as "the Liberator," Simón Bolívar seemed to have achieved his goal.

But his career was like a roller coaster and it was soon on the down side again. The following year, after Napoleon's defeat in Europe, the Spanish royal government moved to recover its New World colony. The better-armed Spanish troops soon regained control of Venezuela and Bolívar went into exile again.

This time he fled to Jamaica in the West Indies. Exhausted and depressed, Bolívar still refused to admit defeat. He expanded his goal beyond Venezuelan independence—now he envisioned all South America free from Spain. He thought deeply about the problems of the continent and what kind of government should replace Spanish rule.

Although Bolívar believed in democracy, he thought the new states of South America needed "paternal governments to heal the sores and wounds of despotism and war." Though he opposed the idea of a monarchy, he wanted a strong leader at the center of power—an idea that would later lead others to call him a dictator.

Despite his temporary setback, he remained optimistic about

the future, writing, "A people that loves freedom will in the end be free. We are a microcosm of the human race. We are a world apart, confined within two oceans, young in arts and sciences, but old as any human society. We are neither Indians nor Europeans, yet we are a part of each." His great dream was "A United Hispanic America" completely free from Spanish rule.

In Haiti, which had earlier won its independence from France, Bolívar picked up supplies and volunteers and departed on his final push to drive out the Spanish. He would be successful this time, for three reasons. First he would get the important support of the *llaneros*, the tough horsemen and fighters of the huge, swampy grassland of northern South America. Second, he recruited a number of European soldiers, veterans of the Napoleonic Wars, to fight for South American freedom. Finally, Bolívar avoided attacking Caracas and directed his attack on a strategic region, the valley of the Orinoco River. Though the valley was a rich cattle-raising region, there were fewer Spanish troops there.

Bolívar's forces moved through the Orinoco valley and captured the city of Angostura (today called Ciudad Bolívar). He made it his base for future operations. Control of the valley gave him sufficient water and supplies for further attacks. Men flocked to his banner, and he led his forces into Colombia for the decisive battle.

It was a rugged march. After slogging through dismal swamps, Bolívar's men climbed the heights to the ridge of the Andes. Many perished in the cold or fell off precipices in the dark. But the Spanish troops hardly expected an army to come rushing

down from the mountains. Bolívar's ragged, starving men surprised and defeated the Spaniards at the Battle of Boyaca on August 7, 1819. It was the turning point in the independence struggle in the north. Within two years, Venezuela, Colombia, and Ecuador were all freed from Spanish rule.

Meanwhile, Bolívar watched with hope and interest the struggle of the countries to the south. There, the independence movement was led by José de San Martín.

San Martín was born in the small Indian village of Yapeyu in today's Argentina on February 25, 1778. He was the son of Juan de San Martín, a Spanish soldier, and his wife Gregoria. Three years after José's birth the family moved to Buenos Aires, capital of the new viceroyalty of La Plata, named for the major river of the region. When José was seven, his father was reassigned to Spain, taking his family with him.

In Spain, José received a good education and followed in his father's footsteps by taking up a career in the army. He fought for Spain in North Africa and Portugal, and distinguished himself for bravery in the battles against Napoleon's army. However, when he heard that the city of Buenos Aires had declared itself independent, feelings of patriotism stirred in his heart. He later wrote:

> In 1811, I was serving in the Spanish army. Twenty years of honorable service had gained for me some consideration in spite of the fact that I was an American; I heard of the revolution in South America; and—forsaking my fortunes and my hopes—I desired only to sacrifice everything to promote the liberty of my native land.

When San Martín arrived in Buenos Aires, the patriot leaders welcomed him, for they had few people with his battle experience. Three hundred men were summoned from throughout the country to be trained by San Martín. They formed the core of his officers during the fighting to come. San Martín inspired his men with the desire to defeat the Spaniards. Dressed in a plain blue uniform, black leather boots, and a two-cornered hat, San Martín filled his soldiers with confidence. Moreover, his kindness and consideration made him well liked by his men.

Hearing that Spanish troops from Montevideo were making their way up the Paraná River, San Martín galloped with his men to meet them on February 3, 1813. Riding at the head of his troops, San Martín had his horse shot from under him. The horse's body pinned him to the ground as the fighting raged all around. A trusty companion stood by him, holding off the enemy. Although outnumbered by the Spanish, San Martín's forces scored a stunning victory.

Although Argentina was now secure, San Martín realized that no part of South America would be safe as long as large numbers of Spanish troops remained anywhere. On the west coast, across the Andes, Peru and Chile were still under Spanish rule, and San Martín developed a daring plan. Because Chile was lightly defended, he decided to cross the Andes into Chile and then move north to the Spanish stronghold of Peru.

San Martín moved to the western Argentine province of Mendoza, which borders Chile. Here he spent three years preparing his troops for the arduous task of climbing the highest mountains in the New World. Volunteers came to San Martín's camp in great numbers. The Chilean patriot General Bernardo O'Higgins joined him. To raise money for the cause, patriotic women donated their wedding rings and jewelry. San Martín set up a factory to produce cloth, and women stitched it up into uniforms. People who knew the region helped prepare maps that would guide the invading force. All the while, San Martín was drilling and training his troops. He was a careful man, and wanted to avoid any possibility of defeat.

In January 1817—a summer month below the equator—San Martín finally led the Army of the Andes westward. Five thousand men joined the march, sometimes using trails so narrow that the horses had to pass single file. Climbing peaks that rose 12,000 feet high, a misstep could send a rider over a cliff to certain death. Because the air was so thin, men faced the danger of mountain sickness. Still, San Martín's careful preparations enabled the army to pass safely through all the potential dangers.

When they entered the Valley of Chile in February, the Army of the Andes surprised and overwhelmed the Spanish troops at Chacabuco. Following this victory San Martín's forces swept north into Santiago, where the people greeted them with joy. Chile was declared independent, with Bernardo O'Higgins as its ruler.

In Chile, with the help of a British mercenary, San Martín built a fleet of ships. Sailing northward, he seized the main Peruvian port of Callao, cutting off the Spanish from supplies by sea. The people of Peru, isolated from the rest of South America, had less enthusiasm for independence. Lima had been the center of Spanish rule and many of its citizens supported the home country. San Martín was willing to wait. Outside Lima, the capital, he proclaimed, "I do not seek military glory, nor am I ambitious for the title of conqueror of Peru: I only wish to free it from oppression. What good would Lima do me if its inhabitants were hostile politically?"

With the town blockaded, merchants soon felt the pinch and some Limeños began to rally to the cause of independence. After soldiers began to desert from the Spanish garrison, panic seized the Spanish officials and their supporters. The viceroy fled Lima with his troops, retreating into the Andes. San Martín entered the city with only a single aide at his side.

On July 28, 1821, in the Plaza of Lima, Peru's independence was proclaimed. Church bells pealed and cannons boomed in celebration. San Martín was named Protector of Peru amid cries of "Long live the Liberator." The joyous mood did not last long. San Martín was a brilliant military commander, but he had no ability or desire to govern. He had gladly turned Chile over to O'Higgins, but in Peru he faced a more difficult problem. Like Bolívar, San Martín had been thinking about the future of a free South America. As he looked at Peru, he believed that it needed a monarchy to keep it stable. He feared the political squabbling that had already begun to appear among the newly independent countries. San Martín was accused of wanting to be king himself, which was untrue. The title "Protector" was the only one he accepted.

Moreover, San Martín's hold on Peru was still threatened as long as the viceroy's troops remained in the mountains. San Martín felt that his own forces were not strong enough to go after them. In this situation, he agreed to meet Bolívar, hoping to find help. When the two men failed to agree, San Martín quietly left the scene, determined to retire from the independence struggle entirely. His decision seems a strange one, since it occurred when final victory was almost within his grasp. But he was ill and had spent much of his adult life fighting both in Europe and America. As he wrote to O'Higgins: "Believe me, my friend, I am tired of being called tyrant, and having it said in all quarters that I wish to become a king, an emperor, or even the devil."

San Martín returned to Peru, where he suggested that the people invite Bolívar to help them in the final push for independence. He performed a final service to Peru by establishing a congress for the nation. He then gave up his title and left the country. That was the end of San Martín's career. Discouraged, he went into exile and died in France in 1850.

As San Martín had hoped, Bolívar now moved south into Peru. On the high plains of Junín, the lances and sabers of his llaneros won the day. The Spanish viceroy surrendered and his remaining troops fled farther into the Andes. Bolívar returned to Lima, leaving his best general, Antônio José Sucre, to win the final battle for independence at Ayacucho in 1824.

Bolívar was hailed and showered with honors and gifts. Bolivia, formerly Southern Peru, was named in his honor. Though he turned down the offer to be ruler of Peru for life, he remained there for a year helping to get a new government on its feet.

He was more concerned with Gran Colombia, a country that he had created, which combined today's nations of Colombia, Venezuela, and Ecuador. When he heard that it was being torn apart by quarrels and disagreement, he returned. However, all his efforts could not prevent Gran Colombia from falling apart. The selfish interests of its different regions were too strong, and the departure of the Spanish left no central authority.

Bolívar, like San Martín, became disillusioned. His great dream of a United Hispanic America was doomed to failure. His health had been hurt by the military campaigns in blizzards and tropical jungles. Critics accused him of wanting to become a dictator, and in 1828, conspirators attempted to assassinate him.

Sick with tuberculosis, Bolívar quit his posts and retired to Santa Marta, a town on the Caribbean Sea. "America is ungovernable," he wrote sadly. "Those who have served the revolution have plowed the sea." Embittered, he died in 1830, only 47 years old.

In 1842, Bolívar's body was brought to Caracas and buried in a grand tomb. After San Martín's death in France eight years later, his heart was returned to Buenos Aires and interred in the city's cathedral. Later generations have forgotten their failures, and revered both men for winning the independence of Spanish South America.

CHAPTER 5

A TOUGH SURVIVOR—
MARIA ANTÔNIA MUNIZ

In 1776, 14-year-old Maria Antônia Muniz picked out her best dress. Maria's aunt, who had raised her, put combs in the girl's hair to hold high her white lace *mantilla,* the long scarf that flowed down nearly to her waist. Maria was getting ready for her wedding to her family's neighbor, Manuel Amaro da Silveira.

Herval, the nearest town to the Muniz ranch in southern Brazil, was too small to have its own church. The young couple and a few friends and relatives rode for two days to a village to find a priest to perform the marriage ceremony. Even then, they had to wait several more days for the priest to return from the rounds he made to ranchos and little settlements in the region.

The delay worried their neighbors back home. This part of the country was claimed by both the Portuguese and the Spaniards, and raids by one side against the other were not unknown. Bandits also roamed the frontier, where law and order were poorly enforced.

Finally, however, the priest returned. The bell of the little church rang out in honor of the newly married couple. When they returned home, their friends and neighbors prepared a wedding feast. Guests raised their glasses in toasts, wishing the couple long life, happiness, and many children. No one could have guessed how those wishes would be fulfilled.

In later years, Maria told the story of her wedding day many times. According to family records, she lived to be well over 100 years old. During her long lifetime Maria experienced both sorrow and joy. She had to be tough to survive in a harsh environment, for Maria and her family were among the pioneers who pushed Brazil's territory into the vast grasslands of the south.

Maria Antônia Muniz was born in 1762 in San Carlos in today's Rio Grande do Sul, the southernmost province of Brazil. Her father and grandfather, poor aristocrats from Portugal, had emigrated to Brazil sometime after the mid-1700s. Drawn by the lure of land in the boundless colony, they settled in the disputed region between the Portuguese and Spanish New World empires. The Portuguese hoped to strengthen their claim to the area by building a fort, the Colonia do Sacramento. Maria's father married the daughter of the fort's commander and the young couple went forth to claim land and cattle in a spot called San Carlos.

The no-man's-land between the two empires was a vast, rolling grassland, well watered and fertile. Wild herds of horses and longhorn cattle—first brought to the New World by the Spanish and Portuguese—roamed there, free for the taking to anyone hardy and tough enough. The sparse population included a few thousand *gauchos*, or cowboys, mainly mestizos and Guaraní Indians. The freewheeling, independent gauchos owed loyalty to no one but themselves. Mounted on horses they had captured and broken, they threw a *boleadora*—three stones held together by a rope—around a cow's legs to bring it down. Beef for food and leather for clothing were all that the gauchos required to survive.

When Maria was an infant, Spanish soldiers swept into the region, and Maria's family fled to the Colonia seeking safety. Spanish troops besieged the fort and finally stormed the town. In the fighting, Maria's mother was killed. Later the Spaniards allowed the Muniz family to return to San Carlos and Maria and her three older brothers spent their early childhood there, cared for by their father and unmarried aunts.

But her father was uncomfortable living in Spanish-claimed land, and soon moved his family farther north to Herval, within the Brazilian border. Though the Muniz homestead had few neighbors, it was fairly close to the large Portuguese settlement at Rio Grande. Soon, however, a joint surveying party drew up a neutral territory between the two empires. Herval and the Muniz family were once again part of a territory that officially belonged to no one.

Because life on the frontier was dangerous, Maria's father kept a gun to protect his family against Spanish soldiers or hostile Charrua Indians. He planted wheat, raised mules, and gathered a herd of cattle by paying gauchos to round them up. In the fall,

Muniz loaded his wheat, meat, and leather on mules, taking them to the town of Rio Grande, where he traded for sugar, salt, and *maté*, the Indian tea drunk throughout the grasslands. Maria eagerly awaited his return, for when the sale went well, he might bring back cloth and ribbons to make a new dress for her saint's feast day, celebrated much like a birthday.

The Portuguese government encouraged more settlers to come to the disputed area to strengthen Portugal's claim against the Spanish. Many new families arrived from Portugal and the Azores, the Portuguese colony off Africa in the Atlantic Ocean. One Azorean family was made up of the Amaro da Silveira brothers, who built a ranch close to the Muniz spread. Maria's father was pleased when one of them showed an interest in his daughter.

After Maria and Manuel married, they built their own home on the top of one of the highest hills in the region. Looking north they could see Portuguese territory and just south, the Spanish lands. Both Maria and Manuel saw this wild region as a land of opportunity even though the life could be harsh. Manuel rounded up cattle and marked them with his own brand. Maria spun thread and wove cloth and did the domestic chores with some help from their slaves.

Over the next 25 years, Maria gave birth to 13 children who lived to adulthood, and more who died young. A large family was an advantage on the frontier. As her boys grew up, they learned to ride, rope, and throw the boleadora as well as any gaucho. Maria's

daughters helped with the chores, and eventually would marry young men in the surrounding area.

Maria clung to the traditions of her Portuguese heritage. She would sing to her children: "'Twas in the village of San Carlos that I was raised and it's noble blood of Portugal I carry in my veins." Every Friday night Maria took out her family Bible, bound with leather and wood, and her sons would read aloud from it. (The boys had been taught to read and write, but the daughters, like Maria herself, received no formal education.) Often she led her family and slaves in singing the *tercia*, or one-third of the rosary. In January, the whole family celebrated the Feast of the Three Wise Men with three days of caroling.

In 1810, Brazil's neighbor to the south, Argentina, revolted against Spanish rule. The Portuguese in Brazil took advantage of the turmoil to raid Spanish settlements and bring back cattle as spoils of war. Herval became a military headquarters for the Portuguese raiders. Maria's family were among the Brazilians who rushed to settle the former Spanish land, extending Brazil's control farther south.

Brazil itself, however, soon experienced important changes. In Europe, Napoleon had invaded Portugal as well as Spain. The Portuguese ruler took refuge in Brazil, and set up his court in Rio de Janeiro, the capital of the colony since 1763. As a result, Brazil's prestige increased, and its people were granted new rights and freedoms. When the king returned to Portugal after Napoleon's defeat, he left his son to rule the colony, advising him, "If Brazil demands independence, grant it, but keep the crown upon your own head." His son followed this advice when the Portuguese government tried to restore control. In 1822, the prince regent declared the independence of Brazil and became Emperor Pedro I. For 67 years Brazil remained an empire, until the monarchy was overthrown in 1889.

On the frontier, Maria and her family paid little heed to developments in the capital. Absorbed in the harsh routine of ranch life, they steadily increased their property. Success was measured in terms of land and cattle and the Amaro da Silveiras prospered from their labors. By the time Maria's husband died in 1824, the family owned about 150 square miles of pasture, 20,000 head of cattle, and about 1,000 horses. The family also now possessed more than 50 slaves.

Maria was 62 when her husband died, proud of her family's success. She would need all her toughness and indomitable spirit to survive the last four decades of her life—times of great tragedy for her family. Maria and Manuel's many sons and sons-in-law had cooperated in expanding the family's land and power, but after Manuel's death, they began to quarrel over the division of his property. As mother and head of the family, Maria retained control of half her husband's estate. She named Domingos Amaro da Silveira, her husband's son by a slave woman, to administer her share. Manuel had always felt great affection for this son and made sure that he learned to read and write. In his will, Manuel freed Domingos from bondage and gave him some lands. The rest of the family also respected Domingos, and he managed the great estate for eight years until he retired in 1832.

Maria lost some of her lands during Brazil's war with Argentina from 1825 to 1828. At the end of the fighting a new nation, called Uruguay, had been created between Brazil and Argentina. Still, the greater part of the Muniz estate was on the Brazilian side of the line. But the Brazilian settlers could no longer acquire new cattle and lands by invading the Spanish-held regions. In fact, after the war Brazilians found themselves the targets of cattle raids from Uruguay. Maria realized that for her family to continue to prosper, they must have a powerful leader. Around that time, her daughter Firmina married Teodoro Braga, a soldier who had distinguished himself in the Argentine war. Maria put Braga in charge of the estate. Her own sons seethed with resentment.

One night in 1833, Maria's eldest and favorite daughter, named after her, arrived at the estate with her children. The younger Maria Antônia hysterically told her mother that a group of masked men had just slit her husband's throat. His murder apparently was part of a feud that had broken out between the Amaro da Silveiras and their in-laws. Maria allowed her daughter and grandchildren to move into the great house on the hill so that they would not have to return to the horrid scene of the crime. Maria moved to another house a few miles away.

Almost as soon as she was settled in her new home, another horror occurred. Her youngest son, jealous that she had chosen Braga to administer the estate, shot him in the back on a hunting trip. The family was falling apart and the hatred fed on itself.

Magnifying the family hatreds was the Farrapo Revolt, which lasted from 1835 to 1845. Brazil was so huge that many of its people felt a greater loyalty to their region than to the nation. In Rio do Sul, where Maria and her family lived, an independence movement broke out. The secessionists, called Farrapos (or "ragamuffins"), believed that the government in Rio de Janeiro did little for them. Others in the region remained loyal to Brazil. Within Maria's family there were partisans on both sides.

One of the Farrapo leaders was Maria's son Vasco. He believed so passionately in the cause that when the Farrapos took over property, he singled out the lands of his widowed sister. In revenge, one of her sons killed Vasco.

The revolt also increased the unfriendly feelings between Maria's two oldest sons, José and Hilario. One day in 1844, Hilario was visiting his mother, now 82 years old. After a meal, he lay down for a nap. Unexpectedly, José arrived with his own son. Their voices awakened Hilario and the two brothers confronted each other. A great silence descended on the room. Then José jumped up crying, "Because of this heartless fiend I am ruined and miserable!" A fight broke out, ending with Hilario and José's son lying dead in a pool of blood. José fled south to Uruguay.

Maria, the formidable matriarch of the family, managed to survive through all these tragedies. In 1855, she went to live with another daughter, Francisca, with whom she spent her last years. Maria never stopped grieving over the deaths of her children—she outlived all but two of them.

Her gnarled old hands still spun thread and wove cloth as she told the family's story to some of her 84 grandchildren, and then to the great-grandchildren as well. She lived to see yet another war in 1865. This time Brazil allied itself with Argentina and Uruguay against Paraguay. Maria watched with sadness as several of her grandsons went off to battle. They won glory for themselves, as well as additional territory for Brazil. But news of the victories meant little to Maria, then over 100 years old. Her memories went back to the hopeful days when her family had been pioneers. She had seen their efforts succeed, but at a terrible cost. Long after Maria's death in 1870, one of the great-grandchildren who had listened to her tales of the family wrote the story of her life as a fitting memorial.

CHAPTER 6

SCHOOL TEACHER TO A NATION—DOMINGO FAUSTINO SARMIENTO

In 1827, 16-year-old Domingo Faustino Sarmiento received word that he had been drafted into the local militia. The region of Argentina where Domingo lived was ruled by Facundo Quiroga, a fierce *caudillo*, or "strong man." In a courageous act of defiance, Sarmiento refused to serve in the militia, and was immediately jailed. When he got out, he joined a band fighting against Quiroga.

Facundo Quiroga was much like other caudillos who flourished in Argentina and throughout South America after independence. Men of great personal charm and popularity, they seized and kept power by forming armies of soldiers who were loyal to them alone. The caudillos attracted followers by appealing to the sufferings of the people. Sometimes a caudillo grew so powerful that he became ruler of the entire country.

In Argentina, many of the caudillos' followers were the gauchos who inhabited the *pampas*, the vast grassland between the Rio Plata and the foothills of the Andes. The caudillos inspired fear and often showed hard-hearted disregard for all civilized values. Such a man was Quiroga.

Sarmiento described Quiroga as an example of "primitive barbarity; he rebelled against control of any sort; his anger was of the wild beast; his jet-black curly hair fell about his forehead and eyes like Medusa's snaky locks; his voice grew hoarse, his glances turned to daggers." When angry, Quiroga was known to have cut a man's throat and kicked another to death. He hacked his own son with an ax because he was talking too much. Within the caudillo's domain, terror took the place of law.

Sarmiento attributed Quiroga's success to the ignorance of his followers and the caudillo's own natural shrewdness. Sarmiento described the following incident:

Some object had been stolen in a company of soldiers, and all attempts to discover the thief had been futile. Quiroga assembled the troop and ordered wands all the same size cut, one for each soldier. He then had the wands distributed among them, and said in a loud, firm voice: "The one whose wand tomorrow is longer than those of the others is the thief." The next day he assembled the troops again, and Quiroga had the wands examined and compared. There was one soldier whose wand was shorter than the others. "You wretch," shouted Facundo in a voice that struck terror to the heart, "you're the thief." And so he was; his confusion revealed his guilt all too clearly. The trick was very simple: the credulous gaucho, fearful that his wand might grow, had cut off a piece. But it requires a certain superiority and certain knowledge of human nature to employ such methods.

In 1832, Sarmiento sought a refuge in Chile, but he would later return to Argentina, eventually becoming its president. Throughout his career, he took a stand against the caudillo system. As a teacher and political leader, Sarmiento represented the highest values of South American civilization.

Domingo Faustino Sarmiento was born February 14, 1811, in western Argentina. Both of his parents' families had been active in the independence movement. Domingo's father had served with San Martín as a mule-driver and took part in the liberation of Chile. He brought his son up listening to tales about the heroic Army of the Andes.

Although Domingo's parents had only a modest income, they ensured that their son got a good education. By the time Domingo was five, he displayed his ability by reading smoothly and quickly in a loud voice. He later remembered: "I was taken from house to house to display my reading, reaping a great harvest of cakes, embraces, and praises which filled me with vanity." He was a bookworm who preferred reading to any kind of play, later admitting that he never learned how to spin a top or bat a ball or fly a kite. His favorite book was the autobiography of Benjamin Franklin. "I felt myself to be Franklin—and why not? I was very poor like him, I studied like him, and following in his footsteps, I might one day come, like him...to make my place in letters and American politics."

Domingo grew up in a time of unrest. After independence, Argentina failed to form a stable government. The country was split between the people of its major city, Buenos Aires, and the caudillos who ruled in the provinces. Those like Sarmiento and his family, who favored a strong centralized government, were known as *unitarios*. The caudillos and their gaucho supporters were *federales*, who wanted to keep power in the hands of local leaders.

In his first exile in Chile, Sarmiento led a peaceful life. He taught school in a village under the shadow of Aconcagua, the tallest peak of the Andes and indeed of all the Americas. For a time he worked as a clerk in a store in Valparaiso, spending half his wages to learn English from a tutor. He got up at two in the morning for his lesson. While working as a mine foreman in 1836, he heard that Quiroga had been killed, and set out for home.

In San Juan, a city in Argentina's northwestern province, Sarmiento opened a school for young women. Throughout his life, he encouraged education for girls. He believed that society would be civilized only when girls as well as boys were educated—for women created the first impression on the minds of their children. In addition, he started his own newspaper, writing hard-hitting articles critical of the government.

By this time, Juan Manuel de Rosas was the leader in Buenos Aires. A caudillo on a larger scale than Quiroga, he seized power in 1829 with the help of his gaucho followers. The son of a wealthy *estanciero*, or ranch owner, from his youth he rode with the gauchos of the pampas and won their respect for his skill on a horse. In power, he and his wife, Doña Maria de la Encarnación, acted against all potential enemies. Doña Maria always wore red, the color of Rosas' supporters. Rosas' troops dressed in red uniforms, and soon, virtually everyone in the capital was sporting a red ribbon or sash. People hung the caudillo's portrait in stores and homes to show their support. It was even placed in churches and carried through the streets in religious processions.

To ensure loyalty, Rosas had a group of spies called the *mazorca*. The word means "ear of corn," a symbol of unity that likened each individual to a single kernel on the ear. When the mazorca discovered dissenters, they were punished swiftly and cruelly. During Rosas' regime, many Argentines fled to neighboring countries. In San Juan, far from the capital, Sarmiento had felt his critical writings would not arouse Rosas' wrath. But they did, and in 1840 Sarmiento once more had to flee to Chile.

During this second exile, Sarmiento became known all over Latin America. He devoted incredible energy to educational projects, preparing the first South American spelling book and publishing educational texts by other writers. He started an educational journal to spread new ideas in teaching and founded a school for teachers, the first of its kind in Latin America.

He also edited a newspaper, where the chapters of his great book, *The Life of Facundo, or Civilization and Barbarism*, first appeared. In this volume, Sarmiento set out to describe the lessons that could be learned from the career of the caudillo he had fought in his youth. The book gives an unflattering portrait of both Quiroga and his followers, the gauchos. Although Sarmiento paid tribute to the gauchos' hardiness and courage, he contrasted their ignorance and lack of culture with the civilized qualities of city dwellers. By an obvious connection, the book was also an attack on Rosas, whose main support also came from the gauchos. When Rosas learned of it, he demanded that the Chilean government return Sarmiento for judgment. However, the Chilean president, who was Sarmiento's personal friend, protected him. The book's beautiful writing made it a classic that was read throughout the Spanish-speaking world.

For all his talents, Sarmiento had his critics. He was a man of vast egotism and conceit. He was often arrogant with those who disagreed with him, and he lacked the skill of compromising. Some Chileans and other Argentine exiles called him *Don Yo*—"Mister I."

In appearance, Sarmiento was an awesome sight. He was very fat and his huge head sat on a bull-like neck. But he did have a sense of humor and laughed at his ugliness as well as his annoying characteristics. A Chilean commented on meeting him:

> Never perhaps has the sun of our continent nourished such a fantastic, ardent, brilliant person, who is, at the same time, a blunderer and a liar. He has a marvelous imagination...with little true talent, no common sense, and his vanity overflows the pampas....This absurd vanity is a perpetual cloud that obscures a sun that occasionally emits splendid rays.

When Sarmiento heard that a revolt against Rosas had broken out, he went to join the rebels. He was present at the Battle of Caseros in 1852, where Rosas was defeated. After the caudillo fled

to exile in Britain, Sarmiento started a newspaper in Buenos Aires. He was elected senator for the province and directed its school system. Then he became governor of his home province of San Juan, putting his ideas into action.

In 1865, the Argentine government named Sarmiento as its ambassador to the United States. Earlier, he had visited the country to study its educational system. On that first trip, he had befriended the influential educator Horace Mann and his wife. His three years as ambassador were happy ones. He traveled extensively, searching for the reasons for the wealth and prosperity of South America's neighbor to the north.

Sailing for home in 1868, Sarmiento landed in Rio de Janeiro and received the news that he had been elected president of his country. Sarmiento's former achievements had earned him prestige and respect, but in the office of president, his personality became something of a drawback. He was snobbish, looking down on the common people and those of mixed blood. He called lower-class Argentines "loafers, drunkards, useless fellows," and always compared them unfavorably with Europeans or people of the United States. Perhaps as a reaction to his own humble origins, he always seemed to want to improve his countrymen. Significantly, one thing about the United States that impressed him most was that even the farmers wore frock coats—or so he claimed.

Even so, Sarmiento's term was a success, for he devoted all his efforts to making Argentina a modern nation. Roads, railways, telegraph lines, and a postal system were built or expanded to tie the capital to the vast lands of the interior. Sarmiento encouraged immigrants from Europe to fill up the empty spaces of the huge land. His efforts began the stream of immigration that would bring over a million new citizens, mainly from Spain and Italy, to Argentina by the end of the century. Sarmiento established the first Argentine census, created a national bank, and launched the first ships of the Argentine navy.

Dearest to his heart, of course, was education. "If I do not advance [popular education]," he assured Congress in 1869, "all of my earlier words and deeds stand as vain ostentation....Failure to do so, now that the way is open, will mean that this Government is impotent to break the tradition of ignorance which is our colonial heritage." At his request, Horace Mann's wife sent 63 women to Argentina to start teacher-training schools. School building and teacher training went forward at a rapid pace. Argentine school enrollment soon surpassed any other Latin American country, and Sarmiento insisted that the schools include gymnasiums, a new idea. He also started a program of adult education.

After leaving the presidency, Sarmiento continued to serve his country as head of the school system. When he died on September 11, 1888, the nation mourned. He was most fondly remembered as Argentina's teacher, and is respected today as the finest Argentine leader of the nineteenth century.

CHAPTER 7

THE TIN KING—SIMÓN I. PATIÑO

Around the year 1892, Simón Patiño kicked the sides of his mule, urging it to go faster. Patiño was in deep trouble. While working as a store clerk in the city of Cochabamba, Bolivia, he had allowed a prospector to buy supplies on credit. Patiño believed the man's claim that he was about to make a huge silver strike. But when the prospector did not return, the owner of the store demanded that Patiño pay back the loan out of his own money. If Patiño could not find the man, he would lose $250, his entire life savings.

Patiño had only a vague idea where to look. The prospector's diggings lay on the eastern slopes of the Andes Mountains, 75 miles west of Cochabamba. As the mule took Patiño ever higher up the lonely peaks, he saw a few armadillos and then only snowbirds or an occasional condor. He melted snow over a fire for water and ate tough strips of lamb jerky called *chalona*, brittle dried corn, and *chunos*—small, frozen potatoes preserved in snow. The mule survived on carefully rationed oats and the blackened *stipa ishu* grass that struggled to grow in the rocky soil.

By the time they reached the 15,000-foot level, both man and mule were feeling the effects of the heights. Patiño's heart raced and his vision blurred; the mule's body jerked from side to side. Only the hope that the prospector might actually have found silver kept Patiño going.

At 17,000 feet, suffering from altitude sickness, Patiño found his prospector, Apac. But the ore that Apac brought out of the ground contained tin, not silver, and Apac did not have the money to repay the loan. "I have lost everything," Patiño lamented. "Before you bought the goods to work the mine I had $250. Now I have nothing." Apac offered to sign over the deed to his mine in payment, and Patiño accepted. His one desperate hope was that the store owner would accept the tin mine as payment for his debt. The two made their way down the heights to Cochabamba.

Weak and thin from the trip, Patiño presented the deed to his boss. When the owner saw that the mine contained only tin, he laughed scornfully and announced that his employee was out of luck. He crossed out the store's name on the deed and wrote in Patiño's. Returning home to his wife, Patiño wept for the first and last time in his life. "We are ruined," he sobbed.

This misfortune turned out to be Patiño's greatest opportunity. The mine, which Patiño had hopefully named La Salvadora ("The Savior"), was the start of an economic empire that would make him the richest man in Bolivia and one of the richest in the world. Patiño would become known as the "Tin King."

Simón Iturri Patiño was born around 1865 in a small town on the high Bolivian plateau called the *altiplano*, about 100 miles from Cochabamba. As a *cholo*, the Bolivian term for a man of Indian and Spanish blood, Patiño had few prospects. Bolivia was a poor, landlocked country with some of the worst rulers in South America. His father was fortunate to have moved up a step, becoming a shoemaker instead of laboring in the fields or mines.

The parish priest gave Simón his only education. Learning to read sparked an intense curiosity in the young cholo's mind. Simón borrowed books anywhere he could and read them eagerly. His imagination was inflamed by the tales of the conquistadors and their search for gold and silver. He learned that Potosí in Bolivia had been the site of the richest silver mine ever discovered. The Spaniards had been digging out its ore with Indian labor for 200 years, but at the time of Simón's childhood, the mine was almost played out. Simón dreamed of finding a new and valuable deposit of the mineral. To learn the business, he started working as a clerk for a silver-mining firm.

Simón had a stroke of good luck when he met Albina Rodríguez, the daughter of poor aristocrats. Though her parents were horrified to hear that she had fallen in love with a brown-skinned cholo, Albina knew her own mind and married him. She alone had faith in Simón's dreams.

When Patiño's job seemed to be going nowhere, Albina suggested he leave the mining company to work in a prosperous hardware store. Here he received his deed to La Salvadora, which he believed to be worthless. Albina thought otherwise. "If that is all

we have," she said, "we must take care of all we have. When you have rested, we will go together to the mine."

Albina borrowed money from friends to outfit the expedition. They hired four Quechua Indian laborers and some llamas to carry their supplies. The little group set out for the mine. Albina brought a book about tin, which she read from by the faint light of fires fed by yareta cactus and dried llama dung. She raised Simón's spirits by telling him of all the things tin was used for—bronze, pewter, kitchenware, candlestick holders, church bells, and drainpipes. Surely someone would want to buy their ore.

When they reached their claim, they built an adobe hut and started work. Using picks and shovels, Simón and his wife worked alongside the Quechuas digging into the mountainside. Six weeks after they had started, their supply of coca leaves ran out and the Quechuas left. As people of the Andes had done for generations, the Quechuas chewed coca leaves to gain energy in the high altitude. Simón too was ready to quit, but Albina insisted that they keep looking. When Simón pointed to the llamas, now thin and weak, and asked how they could carry down the ore if the animals died, Albina responded: "We will carry it on our backs."

Each day they burrowed farther into the hole they had dug, often scraping at the walls with their bare hands and pulling out sacks of dirt and rock. Only at lunchtime, when they went to the surface for a small meal, did they see the sun. On the evening of their 87th day at La Salvadora, they emerged after 11 hours of work. It was snowing, but through the flakes the moon shone on the sacks of rock that Simón and Albina threw on the ground. One large rock glowed brightly, showing the presence of tin. The next morning they returned to the mine to see that they had struck an actual wall of tin. Quickly filling a sack with the rich ore, they returned to Cochabamba.

The cry of "Tin, tin!" may not be as exciting as "Gold, gold!" but Simón was on his way to fulfilling his dream. Just as Albina had predicted, they soon found businessmen who wanted to buy the tin. However, the Patiños needed money to take large quantities of ore out of the mine. They negotiated a loan from an Englishman for $5,000, an unheard-of sum for Patiño. Walking out of the Cochabamba bank with the money draft, Patiño was transformed. He now strode forward with a light step, shoulders erect, and a new look of confidence in his eyes. For the first time he heard himself addressed as *señor*, a term of respect. He stuck out his chest and exclaimed, "Tin does have something."

As the Patiños made their plans for La Salvadora, they feasted on the best llama meat and fresh vegetables, luxuries that they could never afford before. Patiño, once so skimpy and thin, filled out. He bought a suit and tie and discarded his native sandals, or *ajotas*, for his first pair of shoes. Tying the laces, Patiño felt that he had been emancipated from his low class. He began to see himself as one of the socially superior, and another dream formed in his mind. The most respected men's club in Bolivia was the Club Social, the private retreat of Cochabamba's aristocrats, proud of their pure Spanish ancestry. In Simón's mind, he would not be fully accepted until his name appeared on the club's membership list.

The Patiños started to work the La Salvadora mine in a major way. They invested the profits in better equipment, and their wealth continued to grow. But their success brought more prospectors to the area. Criminals tried to steal Patiño's claim and even attempted to kill him. Miners from Chile began working on the other side of the mountain. When they broke through to Patiño's tunnels, fights broke out between the miners deep underground. Patiño led his miners down the shaft with a pistol in one hand and a yareta cactus torch in the other. His forces won the battle, and the Chileans promised to keep out of La Salvadora.

A firm in the United States offered Patiño $350,000 for La Salvadora. Dazzled, he agreed. With such a fabulous sum he could retire and live in luxury for the rest of his life. But Albina was horrified and before he could finish signing the papers, she tore them to pieces. She believed that the mine would be the source of much greater wealth, and she was right.

As the profits continued to grow, Patiño imported more advanced technology, such as electric motors, to work the mines more efficiently. He built a railroad to carry his tin to market. Patiño expanded his business empire by buying banks, utility companies, and other mines. By 1914, he was a millionaire, and in that year World War I broke out in Europe. During the four years of the war, the demand for tin soared and so did his fortune. He was now the wealthiest man in Bolivia. All these ventures brought him immense power with the Bolivian government. Only one thing marred his triumph—he still had not received an invitation to the Club Social.

He started a campaign to realize this dream. With his great sums of money, he traveled the globe to invest in new ventures. He acquired yachts and expensive cars and gave lavish parties. News about the exploits of the country's most famous citizen were front-page stories in Bolivian newspapers. But the members of the Cochabamba Club Social were not impressed.

Patiño thought that becoming a diplomat might help. He demanded that the Bolivian government name him ambassador to France. He felt that the Club Social could not deny admittance to a man in such a prestigious position. In the lavish new embassy in Paris, his children mixed with the high society of Europe. At the same time, he was building a palace for himself in Cochabamba. He called it Miraflores, and displayed his fine art collection in its many rooms. After three years in France, Patiño sailed for Bolivia in 1924, intending to apply for membership in the Club Social without waiting for an invitation.

All Bolivia heard of Patiño's homecoming. He planned a set of banquets to celebrate the opening of his palace, and sent engraved invitations to the city's finest society. One by one, their servants appeared at his door with cards politely declining his invitation. A few days later he received a note that he read aloud to Albina: "The membership committee of the Club Social regret to advise the applicant, Simón Iturri Patiño, that his application presented at the last meeting of members received an unfavorable consideration." Mortified and enraged, Patiño left Bolivia. He would never see it again.

Returning to Paris, he sulked for the next few years, keeping to himself so much that he was dubbed "the hermit of Tin." Even so, Patiño kept informed on what was happening in Bolivia. He always kept a Bolivian flag on his desk, and still had great influence with the government. From 1932 to 1935 Bolivia and Paraguay fought a war over disputed territory. Called the Chaco War, it was a bloody conflict with more than 100,000 casualties. It was Patiño who provided the guns and ammunition used by the Bolivian soldiers. Even so, Paraguay won and Bolivia was left with a huge war debt. Patiño's taxes paid it off.

The one thing that Patiño was not willing to pay for was the labor in his mines. The humble cholo who had achieved his dream of wealth refused to pay a penny more than was necessary to his workers. The miners' wages were kept at starvation level and they were always in debt to the company store, the only place where they could buy food and clothing. The mines were dangerous and many workers suffered illnesses from their underground life.

Some miners had served as soldiers in the Chaco War, and on their return were no longer willing to accept the harsh working conditions. In 1942, the mine workers struck for higher wages and picketed in front of the mines. Government troops opened fire on an unarmed group of demonstrators, killing far more than the official government figure of 19.

The brutal suppression of the strike caused bitter feelings among Bolivians. Some complained that Patiño had used little of his fortune to help Bolivia, spending much of it on a high life-style for himself and his family. Patiño's success was compared to the exploitation of South America by the Spanish, when the wealth of the mines all went to Europe.

Even so, when Patiño died in 1947, Bolivia declared a day of mourning. He was, after all, the most important Bolivian, known the world over as the Tin King. Few had ever risen as far as he had, but the sting of his social rejection was a reminder of South America's unhappy divisions among social classes. Though Patiño had achieved fabulous wealth, he could not cross the final social barrier—the threshold of the Club Social.

CHAPTER 8

A Passionate Voice— Gabriela Mistral

In 1902, 13-year-old Lucila Godoy was already a budding poet. She liked to write little poems, dedicated to her friends, in her school notebook. Though Lucila was shy, she volunteered to take Doña Adelaide Olivares, the blind school director, to and from school each morning and afternoon. Doña Adelaide gave Lucila other duties, putting her in charge of distributing new notebooks to the other students. One day, Lucila told Doña Adelaide that there were not enough notebooks for the class. Irritated, the director scolded her, saying the missing notebooks must have been stolen. Shocked, Lucila made no reply, causing Doña Adelaide to think she must be the thief.

Doña Adelaide assembled the whole school and made Lucila stand up to be accused of stealing. It was a humiliating experience for the sensitive young girl—so much so that she fainted and fell to the floor. That afternoon, as she left school, the other students taunted her all the way home with cries of *Ladrona, ladrona*—"Thief, thief." Afterward, the school discovered that Lucila was completely innocent. But she never returned after that horrible day.

The memory of the incident burned deep into Lucila's soul. It fostered in her a sense that she was different from other people. She turned within herself, seeking comfort and expression in her poetry. Many years later, her poems, written under the pen name Gabriela Mistral, would bring honor to her country, Chile.

Lucila Godoy y Alcayága was born in Vicuña, Chile, on April 7, 1889, the daughter of Jerónimo Godoy and Petronilla Alcayága. She grew up in the small village of Montegrande by the Elqui River, in a region famous for its grapes. Her father, a teacher, had a weakness for drink and left the family when Lucila was three.

Although the family was poor, Lucila regarded her childhood as ideal. She walked along the river, picking pretty stones from the water. On the horizon, she could see the awesome snow-covered Andean peaks that surrounded the valley. At night Lucila lay outside and counted the stars. She learned the scents of nature—new crops growing in the fresh earth in spring, the grapes of midsummer filling with juice that would be made into wine in the fall. In a poem of later years, she wrote:

> O, River Elqui of my childhood
> in which I wade upstream,
> never shall I lose you; side by side
> like two children, we have each other.

When Lucila was almost 10, her mother decided it was time for her to go to school, and sent her back to Vicuña. "I was happy until I left Montegrande," Lucila remembered, "and after that I was never happy again." Her only formal education came from the three years in the school where she was so cruelly humiliated.

Lucila's disgrace was particularly hard to bear, because she felt it came from racial prejudice. Her green eyes and dark skin marked her as a mixture of Indian and Basque, the people who live in the Pyrenees Mountains between Spain and France. Lucila often referred to herself as *una mestiza de vasca* (a Basque mestiza), and sometimes blamed her shortcomings on her mixed race. "I am one of those whose insides, face, and expression are uneasy and irregular...I consider myself to be among the children of that twisted thing that is called a racial experience, or better a racial violence." Although Lucila always condemned racial prejudice, tragically she could not avoid applying it to herself.

Her half-sister Emelina, a teacher, helped Lucila to continue her education. Lucila herself soon began to teach young children in the small villages and towns near Montegrande. In 1906, she found a job as a primary school teacher in the town of La Cantera.

Here Lucila met a young railroad worker named Romelio Ureta and the two fell in love. Romelio was a bit of a dandy, waxing his moustache and wearing pointed shoes of patent leather. He shared Lucila's love of poetry and they spent many hours reading to each other. Then Romelio stopped coming to visit, and Lucila saw him in the street with another woman. She consoled herself by writing poems, and was surprised when two local newspapers accepted some of them for publication.

One day three years later, a policeman arrived to inform Lucila that Romelio Ureta had killed himself. The police had found a postcard from Lucila in his pocket. She never learned why he had carried this memento, but she poured out her grief in six poems that she called "The Sonnets of Death." She put them away without showing them to anyone, for the emotions they expressed were too personal.

But five years later, she was tempted by the announcement of a national poetry contest. Lucila knew that she had never written anything as good as "The Sonnets of Death," and time had softened her pain. However, she could not bear others knowing who had written them, and submitted the poems under a pen name. She picked Gabriela for the angel who bears good news, and Mistral for the cold wind that blows into sunny southern France from the north. Learning that she had won the contest, Lucila attended the award ceremony in disguise while another person read her poetry. From that day in 1914, the name Gabriela Mistral became known all over Chile.

Her new name gave Gabriela the chance to form a new identity. She wrote a friend, "This soul of mine today is far different from the one I had at birth." Friends noticed that she had indeed changed. Her old awkwardness disappeared, replaced by an air of serenity. Because she still believed she was ugly, she always wore plain long dresses and flat shoes. But when she smiled, her face was transformed into that of a happy young woman.

She continued teaching and was named as superintendent of a school system in Punta Arenas, where she lived for two years. The city lies near the southern tip of the long, narrow country of Chile, and the weather there is almost continually stormy. In the winter there is little light and in the summer the sun sets late. The strange, eerie landscape appealed to Gabriela. In Punta Arenas she wrote what she considered her best poem, in which she expressed her deep disappointment at never giving birth to a child.

> A son, a son, a son! I wanted a son of yours
> and mine, in those distant days of burning bliss
> when my bones would tremble at your least murmur
> and my brow would glow with a radiant mist.

Gabriela applied her poetic gifts to her teaching career. She believed that children should read only the best literature, but because she was not impressed with the poems she found for young people, she wrote her own. She wove ancient legends into art that children could appreciate. Some of her poems were humorous, like the following, called "If You'll Just Go To Sleep":

> The blood red rose
> I gathered yesterday,
> and the fire and cinnamon
> of the carnation,
> Bread baked with
> anise seed and honey,
> and a fish in a bowl
> that makes a glow:
> All this is yours,
> baby born of woman,
> if you'll just
> go to sleep.
> A rose, I say!
> I say a carnation!
> Fruit, I say!
> And I say honey!
> A fish that glitters!
> And more, I say—
> if you will only
> sleep till day.

Gabriela's reputation as teacher and poet brought an invitation from the Mexican government to help modernize the country's school and library system. In 1922, Gabriela arrived and fell in love with Mexico, which in turn treated her as a treasure. She received a fine house and a large salary. It was the beginning of a new career for the poet, in which she traveled all over the Americas and Europe. Though she often wrote about women and children and the joys of home life, she never settled for long in one place.

Realizing how much respect other countries had for Mistral's work, the Chilean government named her an honorary consul, allowing her to serve anywhere she chose. In return for her work as a goodwill ambassador for Chile, the government paid for her living expenses. Free from financial worries, Mistral would never again live for more than a year at a time in her homeland.

She spent much time in the United States, for which she had a special affection. It was here, not in her homeland, that her first book of poetry had been published. A professor at Columbia University in New York had discovered her poems and read them in his class for training Spanish teachers. The class was so impressed that they wrote Mistral asking for more. With their help, the first collection of her poems was published. She herself taught in colleges in the United States in the 1930s.

She also lived in France, Portugal, and Spain, continuing to write poetry that now was published in many countries. Throughout the Spanish-speaking world, she was known as La Mistral and honored for her talent. Feeling strongly her obligation to Chile, she strove to correct prejudices about her nation and Latin America in general. In her writing—articles as well as poems—she pleaded for better treatment of women, children, the poor, mestizos, and Indians. She donated the profits from one of her books to orphans of the Spanish Civil War.

When World War II broke out, Mistral left Europe for Brazil, bringing with her a nephew, Juan Miguel, whom she called Yin (the Chinese term for "brightness"). Mistral had raised the slightly deformed child and took him everywhere. After his years abroad,

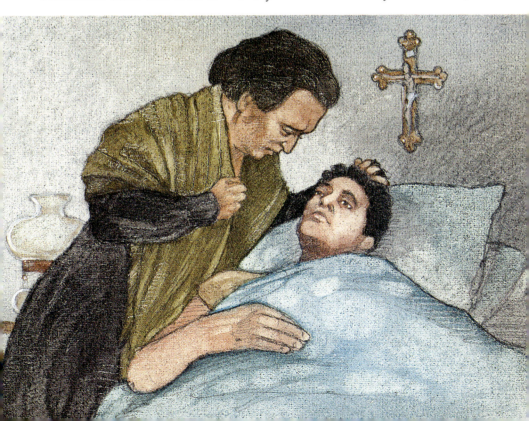

Yin spoke Spanish with an accent and had trouble adjusting. His high school classmates often made fun of him. Gabriela recommended that he leave school but Yin refused.

Then he had an unhappy romance. Remembering her own failed love affair, Gabriela tried to console him, but in 1943 she returned home to find that he had taken poison. During a long, anguished night, Gabriela sat by his bedside as he died in agony.

Mistral almost went mad with grief. She would see Yin in her dreams as if he were still alive. Unable to accept his suicide, she began to speak about an imaginary murder plot. She shut herself up in the big house where they had lived together, and Mistral's friends became concerned for her sanity. They feared that her grief would destroy her. Gabriela's health deteriorated and doctors told her she had diabetes.

She lingered this way for two years. Then word came that she had been awarded the Nobel Prize for Literature for 1945—the first South American to receive that award. Mistral pulled herself together to sail for Stockholm, Sweden, to accept the honor. Dressed in black, the tall, dignified woman gave a short speech in which she accepted the prize on behalf of all Latin America and the "poets of my race."

Mistral never really recovered from the second tragic suicide of a loved one. Though she continued to write, she could not escape her bitterness and pain. In her last years, she seemed to cherish all the bad things of her life and forget the many honors that had come to her. In 1954, she visited Chile for the last time. Her homeland showered her with honors, and Mistral appeared in her shapeless, faded coat to receive every kind of medal that the nation could bestow upon her.

Mistral died in a New York hospital at the beginning of 1957, wasted by ill health and weighing only 90 pounds. Her body was returned to Chile to be buried on a hilltop in Montegrande, the only place in the world where she had found real happiness. She left behind a great gift to the world—her poetry.

CHAPTER 9

THE SONG OF BRAZIL— HEITOR VILLA-LOBOS

In the 1930s, crowds of over 100,000 people filled the stands of Rio de Janeiro's soccer stadium on September 7, Brazil's Independence Day. They came not for a sporting event, but for one of the most astonishing musical spectacles ever presented. On the field below, schoolchildren from all over the country assembled— 40,000 of them. An energetic middle-aged man climbed to the top of a 50-foot tower in the middle of the field. With all eyes on him, he raised a flag, and the children began to sing.

Just to keep such a huge chorus singing together, even for a simple song, would be a difficult task. However, the performances were amazingly complex. Guided by the conductor's flag and by teachers using hand signals, the children sang harmonies and chords that blended together in a wave of beautiful music. By vocalizing letters of the alphabet, they created eerie sound effects. Ten thousand children growling an R made the stadium rumble as if an earthquake were about to hit. Ten thousand more hissing an S made a sound like the rushing wind through an Amazon forest. At a signal, the children clapped their hands and swayed back and forth, each row going in a different direction. A huge orchestra with over a thousand instruments accompanied the chorus, for nothing less could compete with the waves of sound coming from the children's throats. Those who heard the massive performances shook their heads in amazed delight.

Few could understand how children were able to accomplish such a musical feat. When the man on the tower first proposed the idea, he was told it was impossible—music wasn't even taught in ordinary Brazilian schools. But Heitor Villa-Lobos was fond of startling people with the unexpected. The massive choral performances were only part of his lifetime of achievements. Villa-Lobos,

the greatest South American composer, made the world listen to the wonderful music of the people of Brazil.

Heitor Villa-Lobos was born in Rio de Janeiro on March 5, 1887. His parents, Raul and Noemia, raised their eight children in a small apartment over a store. Raul, a librarian, wrote several books on history and enjoyed playing the cello for friends. When Heitor was very young, his father saw that he had a talent for music. The family could not afford lessons, so Raul taught the boy himself. Heitor learned to play piano and clarinet, in addition to the cello. He composed his first song when he was 11.

In that same year, his beloved father died in a smallpox epidemic. Heitor's mother found it difficult to control her talented son. He often skipped school to follow street musicians who played a popular kind of song called *chôro*. The word comes from *chorar*, "to weep," for many of the chôros were sad ballads about disappointed lovers. Heitor took up the guitar and soon played well enough to join the *chôros* groups, sometimes staying out all night in clubs and taverns where the music was performed.

In these sessions, Heitor first heard the folk music that came from little towns and villages in the distant regions of Brazil. When he was 18, he sold some rare books from his father's library so that he could travel into the forests of the Amazon valley. No one knows for certain where he went during most of the next five years. Later, Villa-Lobos liked to tell fabulous stories about his adventures. He claimed to have lived with Indians who ate human flesh, narrowly escaping becoming a meal himself. On another occasion, while imprisoned in a rural jail, he won his release by serenading the chief of police with a saxophone.

What is definitely true is that during these five years Villa-Lobos found the inspiration for his music. Brazil's population was composed of three strains of people: native South Americans, Blacks whose ancestors had been African slaves, and the descendants of Portuguese settlers. Each group had its own music, and Villa-Lobos would combine them in works that are now played throughout the world.

Some of his compositions require instruments that had never before been heard on a concert stage—the *camizão*, a square goatskin drum that Africans devised in Brazil; the *cuiça*, an Indian

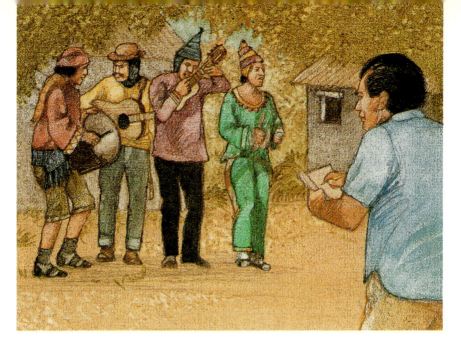

drum that makes sounds like the grunting of an animal; the *cabaça*, a gourd filled with pumpkin seeds; and the *reco-reco*, a short bamboo tube that is played by thumping it on the floor or running a stick down notches cut in the side. Villa-Lobos first heard these instruments deep in the heartland of Brazil.

Through his father's teaching, Villa-Lobos was also steeped in the tradition of European classical music. Feeling he needed more training to fully express the sounds rushing through his head, he returned briefly to Rio. He enrolled in the National Institute of Music, but found the classes boring. When the professors heard a new sound, they looked it up in the textbook. "Aha! It isn't here!" "That is not permissible," they said. Villa-Lobos responded, declaring, "There is no possible growth of music with such men."

Villa-Lobos found work conducting orchestras in restaurants and movie theaters. The silent films of the time were accompanied by music that increased the effect of the action. Villa-Lobos wrote his own music for the films. Here, when he was 31, he got a break that changed his life. Arthur Rubinstein, the great United States pianist, came to Rio on tour. To relax, Rubinstein went to a movie and was startled by what he heard from the orchestra pit. After the show, he approached the conductor to ask where the music had come from. Fearing ridicule, Villa-Lobos admitted that he had written it. Rubinstein invited him to his hotel room to play more of his works.

Rubinstein became Villa-Lobos's lifelong friend and patron. Recognizing the young man's genius, Rubinstein persuaded some wealthy people in Rio to donate funds for Villa-Lobos to perform his work in Europe. The Brazilian government added a small allowance that sent Villa-Lobos to Paris in 1923.

Typically, he arrived smoking a long cigar and declared, "I don't come to learn, I've come to show you what I've done." His dark wavy hair and handsome features made him look like a movie star, and the French press praised him highly. When the first concert of his works was held, critics raved over his use of native instruments and acclaimed him as "a savage from the jungle." Though Villa-Lobos, who spoke perfect French, was probably insulted, he shrewdly used the publicity to promote his music.

By now, he had begun the series of works that he called *chôros*, in memory of the street bands he first played with. They are in fact extremely sophisticated and varied pieces of music. One is played on a single guitar; the largest requires two orchestras and a brass band. Each chôro is intended to create a picture in the mind of the listener. As Villa-Lobos described *Chôro* #10:

> This work represents the state of a civilized human being face to face with nature. He beholds the valleys of the Amazon....He is awed by the vastness and the majesty of the universe. The sky, the waters, the woods, and the kingdom of birds overwhelm him. He feels at one with the life of the people [whose] songs express longing and love.

Now famous, Villa-Lobos spent the next six years performing his new music in most of the major cities of Europe. In 1930, he returned to Brazil, where a revolution had put Getúlio Vargas in power. Though Villa-Lobos avoided involvement in politics, he sympathized with Vargas's aim of bringing the different regions of Brazil under a strong central government. Villa-Lobos thought that music could be a strong force in promoting unity in the multiracial country. He told Vargas, "I can accomplish by means of my art that which you cannot produce with your soldiers."

Vargas agreed to let Villa-Lobos develop a plan for the musical education of Brazilian schoolchildren. The composer's first step was to open a school to train teachers, who then spread out to schools all over the country.

When starting with a new group of children, Villa-Lobos had them sing six words, each in a different tone. The first letters of the words—Bounty, Reality, Amity, Sincerity, Equality, and Loyalty—spelled BRASIL. Villa-Lobos even devised a system that enabled children to create their own melodies on graph paper. The teachers then showed the class how the melody sounded when performed on musical instruments. In 1934, Villa-Lobos demonstrated the success of his work by conducting the first of the Independence Day mass concerts in Rio, which continued until the 1950s.

The decade of the 1930s was an incredibly productive time for Villa-Lobos. He composed the first of the nine works he called *Bachianas Brasileiras*. The title pays homage to the German composer Johann Sebastian Bach, but the music expresses the Brazilian soul. Many other new compositions—symphonies, operas, songs—flowed from his creative mind. Villa-Lobos's office in Rio, where his desk was cluttered with manuscripts and notebooks, was open to anyone who dropped by. He could always find time to show off his expert skill at billiards, at which he was once champion of Rio. As likely as not, a visitor might also be offered a dish of vanilla ice cream, which Villa-Lobos devoured by the quart.

In 1940, when the Brazilian exhibit at the New York World's Fair was about to open, Villa-Lobos was asked to compose a piece for the occasion. He claimed later that to determine the spirit of New York City (which he had never visited), he used the same method he had devised for children. He laid a cut-out photograph of the Manhattan skyline on a piece of graph paper and let the shapes of the buildings determine the notes. The result, the "New York Sky-Line Melody," performed by orchestra and chorus, was broadcast via radio from Rio to New York.

Villa-Lobos made his first concert tour of the United States in 1944. He received such acclaim that he returned every year until his death. On one of his trips to New York, he was operated on for cancer, caused by his continual cigar-smoking. For the last 11 years of his life he was in constant pain, but continued his amazing output of work until his death in Rio in 1959. During his lifetime, he is thought to have written well over a thousand musical compositions. He gave away many of the original scores and others were stolen, so that a complete recording of Villa-Lobos's work has never been made.

CHAPTER 10

"I WILL BE SOMEBODY"— EVITA PERÓN

On January 22, 1944, a crowd gathered outside a theater in Buenos Aires, Argentina, to watch the rich and famous emerge from their limousines. The stars of Argentina's entertainment world were presenting a gala charity performance for the victims of an earthquake that had devastated the western part of the country. Evita Duarte, a radio actress, smiled and waved briefly to the crowd on her way inside. No one knew that this evening would change her life, and all of Argentina as well.

As Evita entered the theater, she noticed a tall, dark, middle-aged man surrounded by beautiful actresses. She recognized him as Juan Domingo Perón, one of the military officers who had overthrown the civilian government and seized power the year before. Evita watched as Perón took a seat next to Argentina's greatest tango singer, Libertad la Marque. When it was Libertad's turn to entertain, Evita slipped into the vacant seat next to Perón. After Libertad finished her song, Evita led the crowd in wild applause, compelling Libertad to sing one encore after another. Meanwhile, Evita took the opportunity to become better acquainted with Perón.

Within weeks, Evita Duarte and Juan Perón were seen arm-in-arm everywhere. The petite blond actress had conquered the heart of the suave, striking Perón. It was the beginning of a political alliance that would change Argentina.

María Eva Duarte was born May 7, 1919, in Los Toldos, a small town in the province of Buenos Aires. Her parents were not married, and her father, Juan Duarte, lived with his legal wife and family. María Eva grew up with her mother, Juana Ibarguen, three older sisters, and a brother—all Duarte's children. Their father provided money for his "second family's" support.

When Eva, as she was called, was seven, her father died. Juana wanted to pay her respects to the man who had fathered her children, but Duarte's legal wife refused to allow it. It took the order of a friend in the local government to enable Juana and her children to attend the funeral. On a cold July day (winter below the equator), Eva held her mother's hand as they filed past the open coffin. The little girl was so terrified by the glares of Señora Duarte and her family that she dared not speak.

Eva's family was now poor and there were few job opportunities for an uneducated woman like Juana. She took her family to the town of Junín, where she opened a boardinghouse. Though Eva's brother and sisters did well in school and found good jobs, Eva was a problem. Not a good student, her only interests were fan magazines and the radio programs that came from Buenos Aires. Listening to the tango bands playing in the grand hotels of the capital, Eva dreamed of a more exciting life. As she looked at the pictures of stars in her movie magazines, she decided to be an actress.

In January 1935, when she was 15, Eva left home for Buenos Aires. She was one of thousands of Argentines who made the trek to the capital each year to seek their fortunes in the prosperous city. Calling herself Evita ("little Eva"), she made the rounds of movie studios and radio stations, auditioning for bit parts. Times were tough in those Depression years, and Evita often went hungry. Still she was determined, often telling her friends, "I will be somebody. I can just feel it." Then, in 1939, she got her big break by landing a role in a radio soap opera. The audience loved her, and three years later Evita became the star of her own show.

Able to indulge herself for the first time, she bought high-fashion clothes and expensive jewelry. The petite brunette changed her hair color to blond and rented an apartment in a fashionable section of Buenos Aires. Evita was 25 when she met Juan Domingo Perón. He was 48, and a widower. It was a political asset for him to appear in public with the beautiful star. They had two things in common: a poverty-stricken childhood and driving ambition.

Perón had risen through the military to the rank of colonel. After the 1943 military coup, he was named head of the Ministry of Labor, a position that he used to increase his popularity. Perón backed the labor unions and urged employers to raise wages and benefits. At the same time, he placed his own followers in the unions' leadership. The gains Perón won for labor gave him a strong group of supporters. To workers who received benefits on a scale they had never enjoyed before, Perón seemed a real friend.

Meanwhile, Evita began a radio series called "Toward a Better Future," in which she spoke of the need for sacrifice and patriotism. Her dramatic training helped her sway the audience with emotional speeches, in which she trumpeted the achievements of Juan Perón. It was said that Perón stopped work each Wednesday and Friday at 7 p.m. so that he would not miss a word of her broadcasts.

By 1945, the military leaders saw Perón's growing popularity as a threat. When one of them criticized Perón for "chasing after the actress Eva Duarte," he replied flippantly, "Well, what do you expect me to chase, actors?" Now the army moved to stop him. In October, Perón was forced to resign all his posts, and Evita was fired from her radio job. Worried about their safety, the two of them decided to flee the capital. The military captured Perón and threw him in jail, but decided that Evita was not worth worrying about and let her go.

That was a mistake. Mustering all her strength and will, Evita moved through the working-class neighborhoods organizing a demonstration in Perón's support. Word spread throughout the country, and soon people were flocking to the city for the "Day of Days." On October 17, a huge crowd filled the Plaza de Mayo in the heart of Buenos Aires. Stores closed and factories ground to a halt

as people left their jobs to attend. Carrying banners and posters, they chanted Perón's name, calling for his freedom.

The government panicked and, to pacify the crowd, allowed Perón to speak. When he appeared, the workers went wild. Perón warmly thanked the people for coming to show their support in his time of need. The government was forced to release him.

Perón realized that he owed his triumph to Evita. A few days later the couple were married in a private ceremony. Soon afterward Perón announced that he would run for president in the elections scheduled for the next year. Argentina was treated to one of the most unusual campaigns it had ever seen. Evita was as much a part of the campaign as her husband. In the past, politicians had courted the wealthy ranchers, landowners, and industrialists. Perón and Evita traveled through the country by train, making frequent stops, and appealing to the grievances of laborers, who were contemptuously called *descamisados*, or "shirtless ones," by the elite.

Perón removed his own shirt to work alongside field hands; photographs of such scenes, displaying Perón's muscular physique, were distributed throughout the country. Evita, on the other hand, appeared in her finest clothes, swathed with jewels. Speaking before enormous, cheering crowds, she reminded them that she had once been poor. She knew how to rouse the people's hopes and dreams, for she had once felt them herself. After the votes were counted, Perón won the presidency.

The wives of Argentine presidents were expected to be dignified, adoring, and silent. On Inauguration Day, Evita showed that she would not be a traditional first lady. She wore a low-cut designer gown instead of the modest one customary for the occasion. The archbishop who sat next to her at the banquet that evening was so embarrassed that he kept his eyes firmly glued on his plate.

If Evita believed that being First Lady would bring her acceptance by the social elite of Argentina, she soon learned otherwise. Traditionally the first lady was asked to head the Beneficia, a charitable organization. But the upper-class women who ran the group showed their disapproval by withholding the honor. When Evita boldly demanded to know why, they said she was too young. So Evita suggested that perhaps her own mother could head the Beneficia. That was also unacceptable, so Evita started her own charity organization—the Eva Perón Foundation.

Evita was not shy about asking for contributions to her foundation. Business leaders and wealthy landowners responded generously, feeling that it was not healthy to turn down the First Lady's requests. At its high point, the Eva Perón Foundation took in more than $50 million a year. Evita was in sole charge of it, and because it was a charitable foundation, it did not have to pay taxes nor account for how its funds were spent.

Quite a bit of the money went for well publicized good works. Evita appeared at the dedications of hospitals, schools, and playgrounds. She could be generous in odd ways. Sometimes, poor families would be brought to the capital for a stay at the most expensive and luxurious hotels. Then they would return home, with the memory of a taste of wealth.

Evita took an office at the Ministry of Labor and virtually ran the department. Her door was open to anyone, and people from all over the country came to ask her help. She kept a stack of 100-peso bills on her desk and would slip a few to visitors whose stories touched her heart. The country's poor regarded her as a holy woman, virtually the reincarnation of the Virgin Mary. Some came to be cured from illnesses, and Evita would write out a prescription for medicine, even though she had no medical training. Other Argentines, of the middle and upper classes, viewed Evita with disgust, comparing her to Doña Encarnación, the wife of the caudillo Juan Manuel Rosas.

Evita was not deterred by criticism. She formed the Women's Peronista Party, which worked for women's rights. In 1947, through her influence, Argentine women were granted full privileges of citizenship and given the right to vote. Evita also campaigned for women to receive equal pay with men in the workplace. She even called for wives and mothers to receive wages for the work they did at home. In these reforms she was a woman ahead of her time.

The darker side of the Perón regime was corruption and a refusal to respect the right to disagree. Evita gave her relatives government posts. No one knows how much of the Evita Perón Fund went into the pockets of Juan and Evita and their relatives, but they lived lavishly. The Peróns also controlled the press and bought newspapers that were critical of them. Opponents of the regime were imprisoned or exiled.

In 1951, Evita experienced a setback. The constitution had

been changed to allow Perón to succeed himself in office. When he began his reelection campaign, he announced that Evita would be his running mate as vice president. The news caused a storm of protest. Fearing that Evita might become president, the army, which still held considerable power, informed Perón that the decision was unacceptable.

Perón persuaded Evita to leave the ticket, and she gave a long, emotional speech over the radio. "I have wanted and I want nothing for myself," she said. "My glory is and always will be the shield of Perón and the banner of my people, and even if I leave shreds of my life on the wayside I know that you will gather them up in my name and carry them like a flag of victory." Evita said she was removing her name from the ballot because she was only 28—too young to assume the office. Everyone knew she had cut four years off her real age to preserve her pride.

The blow took its toll on Evita, and shortly before the election she went into a hospital to be treated for cancer. As she went into surgery, people gathered at open-air masses throughout Argentina to pray for her recovery. Although Evita could not take part in the campaign, her picture was part of all Peronista rallies. Juan Perón won the election with a greater majority than before.

Evita's health never recovered and as she lay dying, Perón showered her with honors, giving her the titles "Spiritual Leader of the Nation" and "Capitana Evita." Her death at age 33, on July 26, 1952, caused a wild outpouring of grief. Mobs swarmed to her funeral to catch a glimpse of her body. The hysteria was so great that eight people were trampled to death and many more injured. Perón had her body embalmed and put on display.

Perón himself was never the same after Evita's death, and his popularity dimmed. In 1955, he was ousted by the military and sent into exile. He returned in 1973 to win the presidency with a new wife, Isabelita, as his vice president. When he died in office, she became the first and so far only woman president of Argentina. Isabelita, however, was a failure because she lacked political skills.

Eva Duarte Perón today is deeply revered in Argentina. Even in death she divided the nation. Some saw her as a saint, others as a devil. Her very real achievements were marred by her desire for power and wealth. She remains one of the most fascinating and controversial women in South American history.

CHAPTER 11

"The Black Pearl"—Pelé

The stadium in Stockholm, Sweden, was more than filled for the final match of the 1958 World Cup of soccer. Sixty thousand fans jammed their way into an arena built to hold 50,000, hoping to see Sweden's national team win its first world title. Out of 53 teams that had begun the tournament, only Sweden and Brazil remained. The crowd roared when Sweden scored the first goal of the contest.

The Swedish coach had predicted that if his team scored first, they would win. He knew that the Brazilian players had a tendency to become disorganized when they fell behind. One of the Brazilians, called by his nickname Pelé, was only 17—the youngest player ever to compete in the World Cup finals. With so little experience, he would certainly crack under the pressure.

But Pelé was remarkably calm, even though an injured right knee made every step painful. He reminded himself that his parents, like virtually everybody else in Brazil, were listening on the radio. Determined to make them proud, he ran up and down the field with a furious pace, inspiring his teammates to play harder. Brazil tied the game and then went ahead just before halftime.

In the second half, Pelé put on a display of soccer skill that stunned spectators and opponents alike. When the ball sailed through the air, Pelé jumped high above the other players to knock it toward the goal with his head. He controlled his body like an acrobat, turning and twisting in the air as if defying gravity. With a flip of his foot, he sent the ball flying over the head of the Swedish goaltender. Sweden fought back, scoring a second time. Then one of Pelé's teammates knocked Brazil's fourth goal into the net.

The best was yet to come. Those who were in the stadium never forgot what they saw. As Pelé stood with his back to the goal, a teammate sent a pass in his direction. Pelé leaped up and cradled the ball against his body. He let it roll down his left leg and then abruptly kicked it over his shoulder. Before the ball came down,

Pelé had whirled around and knocked it straight past the goalie with his right foot. The play was so spectacular that the Swedish fans began to chant, "Pelé, Pelé!" Later the Swedish goaltender joined in the praise. "I have never seen anything like that before and I doubt if I ever will see a goal scored like that again. It was unbelievable."

The Brazilian team returned home as national heroes. Newspapers dubbed Pelé "The Black Pearl." In a country that was soccer mad, Pelé was the king of the game. He would go on to become the greatest superstar of the most popular sport in the world.

Pelé was born Edson Arantes do Nascimento on October 23, 1940, in the small town of Três Coraçoes ("Three Hearts") in Minas Gerais state. He was the first son of Dondinho, a soccer player, and his wife Celeste. Dondinho was playing with his team in another city when Edson was born. On first seeing his infant son, he exclaimed, "Look at his legs. He is going to be a great soccer player." Celeste was not pleased by the remark, for she wanted her son to be anything but a soccer player. She always feared that her husband would be hurt in a game, and blamed the sport for his long absences from home and the family's lack of money.

When Edson was about five, his father signed with another team, in Bauru. The family, now including a younger brother and sister, moved there. Edson spent a happy childhood running with the other children in his crowded neighborhood. Watching the older boys playing soccer, he tried to force his way into the games. The children played on the sidewalks, with old tin cans serving as goalposts. Since there was no money for a real soccer ball, they used a grapefruit or socks filled with rags. Still Edson learned many tricks, such as keeping the ball in the air by bouncing it off his knees or other parts of the body. (In soccer, no one but the goalie can touch the ball with his hands.) Edson was learning the skills of moving the ball, passing, and "heading" that would make him the game's greatest player.

It was in these early days that the boys dubbed him Pelé. The name has no meaning in Portuguese and at first Edson hated it. He recalled,

> The harder I tried to make them stop calling me Pelé the more they insisted on calling me by that name....I used to go home crying to my father, but he told me that I shouldn't be so insulted by that name since many of the top Brazilian players had nicknames that had nothing to do with their regular names. I guess after a while I accepted the name but even today my real friends call me Edson.

When Pelé began to attend school, he found it difficult to sit still at a desk for the whole day. All he wanted to do was to play soccer with the older boys during recess. Often he played hooky and in fourth grade, he quit school. He became a cobbler's apprentice, earning two dollars a month.

In his free time, Pelé joined an informal soccer team. They called themselves the September 7s after the street on which they lived, which was named for the anniversary of Brazilian independence. By selling roasted peanuts in front of the local movie house, the boys bought used uniforms and a real ball. It was a chance to play regularly and Pelé was thrilled. His many natural skills, great speed, and agility, began to show. When Pelé was 12, a former soccer professional came to Bauru to start a junior league. Pelé's father took him to the tryouts, and Pelé was the first player chosen.

Now Pelé had a chance to play a regulation game. He had a sharp new uniform and, for the first time, real shoes with cleats. His coach began to teach Pelé the strategy and tactics of professional soccer. Previously, he had used only his right foot for ball handling; now he learned to use the left as well.

Scouts spotted Pelé, and when he was 14, he was invited to join the Santos professional team. Pelé set out alone on a long train ride, wearing his first pair of long pants and carrying the bananas and bread his mother had packed. Santos is the port for Brazil's largest city, São Paulo. Life in the huge city was very different from Bauru, and Pelé was homesick. He lived in a boardinghouse with other team members, who often treated him like an errand boy. Between games and practices, he went back to school to pick up the education he lacked. He would play with Santos for 18 years.

The team traveled to many of Brazil's other cities. Pelé was awed when he walked onto the field of Macarena Stadium in Rio, built during the presidency of Getúlio Vargas. It is the largest stadium in the world, seating 200,000 people. Before long, the fans in other cities turned out just to see this remarkable new player. In one memorable game against Portugal, a country the Brazilians always wanted to beat, Pelé thrilled the crowd by scoring three goals. Soccer is a low-scoring game, and a goal is usually rarer than a home run in baseball.

Though only 17, Pelé was picked for the Brazilian team that would play for the World Cup. However, before the team left he injured his knee in a practice game. This worried Pelé because after his father had suffered a similar injury, he was never able to play professionally again. Doctors massaged and treated the knee but it still was not back to normal when the time came to leave for Stockholm. Yet he starred in the World Cup matches and returned to Brazil a hero. Even his mother, Celeste, who had refused to attend his games because she feared seeing him injured, now started to watch her famous son play on television.

When Pelé turned 18, he was inducted into the army for his one year of compulsory service. Since it was peacetime, he was allowed to keep playing for the Santos team, but also had to play with the Army team. The grueling schedule was incredible—he once played seven games in 14 days—particularly because Pelé lost between four and six pounds every game. But by playing so many games, he set new scoring records. In 1959 he scored 127 goals—more than any player ever had in a single year.

In 1962, Pelé helped the Brazilian team win the World Cup again. Brazilians were thrilled, but now offers came pouring in to ask Pelé to play for teams in other countries. The Santos team was offered more than a million dollars for his contract. But Brazil declared Pelé a "national treasure," and passed a law that made it illegal for him to play for any other country in the prime of his career. Santos signed him to a new contract that made him the highest-paid athlete in the world.

Pelé was so famous that he could not go anywhere without being recognized. Despite the admiration of the crowds, he remained modest about his talents, believing that they were a special gift from God. "I feel the divine gift to make something out of nothing," he said,

> You need balance and speed of mind and strength. But there is something else that God has given me. It's an extra instinct I have for the game. Sometimes I can take the ball and no one can foresee any danger. And then, two or three seconds later, there is a goal. This doesn't make me proud, it makes me humble because it is a talent that God gave me.

The 1966 World Cup aroused great excitement in Brazil, because if its national team won a third time, it would get to keep the cup. No country had ever won three times. However, the Brazilian team was divided by jealousy and quarreling. In addition, the play of world competition had become much rougher. Pelé's style was graceful, almost like a ballet dancer's, but other teams now recruited players who tried to win through violent physical contact. As the competition began, it became clear that they were gunning for Pelé. In the first game against Bulgaria, Pelé was injured so badly that he could not play in the next one. In his next game, against Portugal, Pelé had to be carried off the field on a stretcher. Brazil lost the championship, and Pelé said afterward: "For me there will be no more World Cups. Soccer has been distorted by violence and destructive tactics. I don't want to end up an invalid."

Still, after Pelé healed he resumed playing for Santos. In November 1969, a huge crowd poured into Rio's Macarena Stadium. By now Pelé had scored 999 goals, more than any other player in South American history, and everyone wanted to see number 1,000. Despite a pouring rain, the crowd was not disappointed. Pelé was tripped on his way toward the goal, and was allowed to take a free penalty kick. Pelé faced the goalie one-on-one, faked once, twice—and then booted the ball into the net! The crowd cheered so wildly that the game had to be stopped to let Pelé run a victory lap around the stadium.

Despite his earlier pledge, Pelé agreed to play in the World Cup tournament in 1970. Brazil's team was a strong one that year, and he saw the chance to avenge the defeat that he experienced four years earlier. This time the matches were in Mexico City. The Brazilians faced a tough Italian squad in the finals, but Pelé scored with a fantastic headshot to lead his team to victory. Brazil took home the Cup, as the first country ever to win it three times.

Pelé seemed to have achieved all that was possible in the sport. By now he was a millionaire, had a wife and young son, and after over 1,200 games his body was tired. He announced his retirement from the Santos team after the 1974 season. He finished his career with 1,216 goals—still an all time world record.

Just six months later, however, Pelé signed with the New York Cosmos, a team in the newly formed North American Soccer League. He was paid a tremendous salary, but he said the real reason was that he wanted to make soccer popular in the United States. Pelé's presence sparked a boom of interest in the sport, but when he departed after three years, the soccer league ended.

In Brazil, Pelé remained in the public eye. He starred in several movies, but turned down an offer to coach the Santos team. He had always loved to sing and play the guitar, and recorded a song called "Obrigado Pelé" (Pelé Says Thank You), which became a hit. The song thanked his family, parents, the country, and the world for his great success.

Recently Pelé has become interested in politics, wanting to do more to change his country. "Brazil," he says, "is a very rich country. It has everything in resources, but there is terrible poverty there and that is unacceptable." At his 50th birthday party in 1990, he announced his hope to use his fame to do something about this. The world may not have seen the end of the career of Edson Arantes do Nascimento.

CHAPTER 12

"Daily Miracles"— Gabriel García Márquez

Read the first words of one of the greatest novels of the 20th century:

> Many years later, as he faced the firing squad, Colonel Aureliano Buendía was to remember that distant afternoon when his father took him to discover ice. At that time Macondo was a village of twenty adobe houses, built on the bank of a river of clear water that ran along a bed of polished stones, which were white and enormous, like prehistoric eggs. The world was so recent that many things lacked names, and in order to indicate them it was necessary to point. Every year during the month of March a family of ragged gypsies would set up their tents near the village, and with a great uproar of pipes and kettledrums they would display new inventions....
>
> [The Buendía children] insisted so much that José Arcadio Buendía paid the thirty reales and led them into the center of the tent, where there was a giant with a hairy torso and a shaved head, with a copper ring in his nose and a heavy iron chain on his ankle, watching over a pirate chest. When it was opened by the giant, the chest gave off a glacial exhalation. Inside there was only an enormous, transparent block with infinite internal needles in which the light of the sunset was broken up into colored stars. Disconcerted, knowing that the children were watching for an immediate explanation, José Arcadio Buendía ventured a murmur:
>
> "It's the largest diamond in the world."
>
> "No," the gypsy countered. "It's ice."
>
> José Arcadio Buendía, without understanding, stretched out his hand toward the cake, but the giant moved it away. "Five reales more to touch it," he said. José Arcadio Buendía paid them and put his hand on the ice and held it there for several minutes as his heart filled with fear and jubilation at the contact with mystery. Without knowing what to say, he paid ten reales more so that his sons could have that prodigious experience.

Little José Arcadio refused to touch it. Aureliano, on the other hand, took a step forward and put his hand on it, withdrawing it immediately. "It's boiling," he exclaimed, startled. But his father paid no attention to him. Intoxicated by the evidence of the miracle...he paid another five reales and with his hand on the cake, as if giving testimony on the holy scriptures, he exclaimed:

"This is the great invention of our time."

This is just a small sample of the wonders of Gabriel García Márquez's novel *One Hundred Years of Solitude*. Set in the fictional town of Macondo, the book tells the story of the Buendía family. The greatest of all South American novels, it plunges its readers into a world of mysteries and adventures and magic.

Gabriel García Márquez was born March 6, 1928, in the town of Aracataca, Colombia. Set in a tropical region of torrential rains, Aracataca is only 50 miles from the Caribbean. Early in the 1920s, banana plantations were started in the area, bringing an influx of workers seeking their fortunes. Among them was Gabriel Eligio García, his father. The older residents of the town looked down on the newcomers, calling them *las hojarascas*, or "fallen leaves," and therefore trash. When one of those leaves, Gabriel Eligio, married Luisa Santiaga Márquez, the daughter of one of Aracataca's first families, her parents did not approve.

The banana boom soon faded, and Gabriel Eligio found a job as a telegraph operator in a coastal town, taking his wife with him. They left their son in the care of his maternal grandparents in Aracataca. Gabriel García Márquez grew up in their decaying old house, where it was said that ghosts walked among the living. "In that house," Gabriel wrote,

> there was an empty room where Aunt Petra had died. There was an empty room where Uncle Lazarus had died. And so, at night, you couldn't walk in that house, because the dead outnumbered the living. They would sit me down at six in the evening, in a corner, and they would say to me: "Don't move from here, because, if you do, Aunt Petra, who is in her room, will come, or Uncle Lazarus..." I always stayed sitting.

Gabriel's grandfather was an imposing figure, "the biggest eater I can remember." The boy loved to listen to him tell of his days as an officer in the bloody Colombian civil war, known as the War of a Thousand Days. His grandmother was a storyteller too, weaving strange tales of miraculous events, providing explanations and details that made them appear completely logical. "It's possible to get away with anything," García Márquez once wrote, "as long as you make it believable. That is something my grandmother taught me." Gabriel stored up these memories and stories in his mind, and one day they would reappear in his writings.

After his grandparents died, Gabriel went to live with his parents. They soon sent him off to boarding school. When he was 14, he traveled to Bogotá, the capital of Colombia, unprepared for what he saw. García Márquez had lived in the part of Colombia that lies along the Caribbean coast. The culture of this region is a mix of Spanish, African, and Indian components and life has an easygoing quality.

Bogotá was very different. Four centuries before, in 1538, the conquistador Jiménez de Quesada, on his search for El Dorado, had reached Bacata, home of the Zipa, the high chief of the Muisca Indians. Though de Quesada did not realize it, the Zipa was the Gilded Man he had been seeking. Each new Zipa, in his consecration ceremony, was coated in gold dust, and both gold and emeralds were tossed into a nearby lagoon as an offering to the gods. The Spanish looted the treasure they found, slaughtered the inhabitants, and renamed the city Santa Fé de Bogotá. It became the capital of the viceroy of New Granada.

When young García Márquez arrived, Bogotá still resembled a medieval city in Spain. As he recalled:

> I arrived from Barranquilla in 1943 at five o'clock in the afternoon...and that was the most terrible experience in the whole of my youth. Bogotá was dismal, smelling of soot, and the drizzle fell unceasingly, and men dressed in black, with black hats, went stumbling through the streets....You only saw a woman occasionally, since they were not allowed in the majority of public places.

After graduation from high school in 1946, García Márquez enrolled in the University of Bogotá law school. His desire for a law degree was halfhearted, and he began to write articles for a Bogotá newspaper. He felt the urge to use his pen to work for a more just society. In his second year of law school, the popular Liberal politician Jorge Gaitán was assassinated. Outraged, thousands of people took to the streets, protesting and looting stores. The police and army fired into the crowds, killing over a thousand people. This was the start of what Colombians call *La Violencia*. For the next ten years a war raged between partisans of the Liberal and Conservative parties. It was like the War of the Thousand Days all over again. More than a quarter of a million Colombians died during the fighting.

The university was closed and Gabriel returned to the Caribbean part of Colombia, where the violence was far less severe. He continued to write, beginning a novel which he titled *La Hojarasca*, (the United States edition is called *Leaf Storm*) in which his mythical town of Macondo appeared for the first time. *Macondo* is the Bantu word for "banana," reflecting the African heritage that northern Colombia shares with the Caribbean countries.

It took García Márquez seven years to get the book published. In that same year, he got into trouble with the Colombian government for a series of articles he had written about the shipwreck of a navy destroyer. The country had praised the lone survivor of the wreck as a hero. But García Márquez's articles showed that the destroyer had been on a smuggling mission, and that it had sunk because it was overloaded with booty. To protect García Márquez from acts of revenge, his newspaper sent him to Europe as a reporter.

There he wrote two more novels. One, *In Evil Hour*, is set in a small town during La Violencia. It shows how the effects of the country's internal strife have seeped into daily life. A man with a terrible toothache cannot go to a dentist because the only one in town belongs to the opposite political party. Márquez's other novel, *No One Writes to the Colonel*, is about a veteran of the War of a Thousand Days who spends his days waiting for the mail that will bring his pension check.

None of his first three novels earned García Márquez any money. The salary that the newspaper paid him was tiny, and he was often in need of cash. Once he was reduced to collecting empty bottles to sell. "For three years I lived by daily miracles," he recalled. "This produced tremendous bitterness in me....But if I hadn't lived those years I probably wouldn't be a writer."

His journalistic career took him back to Colombia, and then to other Latin American countries. While he was living in Mexico City in January 1965, the idea for *One Hundred Years of Solitude* came to him. He went home and told his wife not to disturb him for any reason. For 18 months, he worked for eight to ten hours each day on his manuscript. During this time, he never asked his wife about how she was dealing with such everyday problems as living expenses. When he finished she told him that they were in debt for $12,000. García Márquez shrugged; he felt that this novel would be a great success, and he was right.

One Hundred Years of Solitude tells the history of Macondo from its founding to its final destruction. Six generations of the Buendía family live out their fabulous careers in the novel's pages. To tell the story, García Márquez adopted a new style, called magical realism. Just like his grandmother's stories, it combined fairy-tale fantasy with realistic events to portray a deeper, mythical version of truth. Strange things happen in Macondo: it rains for four years, eleven months and two days; whenever a priest drinks chocolate, he rises into the air; and yellow flowers drop from the sky when the patriarch of the Buendía clan dies. The world of Macondo is as fantastic as the history of South America itself. Yet García Márquez makes his readers believe that it really exists.

The dreams of the Buendía clan are as outsized as those of the

conquistadors. When José Arcadio Buendía sees a magnet for the first time, he immediately imagines using it to find gold. Though he is told this is impossible, he trades his mule and goats for two magnets. "Very soon we'll have gold enough and more to pave the floors of the house," he promises his wife. The only thing he finds is a sixteenth-century suit of armor with a skeleton inside. Around its neck is a locket containing a lock of a woman's hair—a reminder of the failed dreams of the past.

García Márquez's great book is as appealing as the ghostly tales he heard years before in his grandparents' home. From the time of the novel's first publication in 1967, it has been a huge success in every country where it has appeared. In 1982, García Márquez won the Nobel Prize for Literature. His triumph has sparked an interest around the world in other modern South American writers as well.

Known to his friends as "Gabo," García Márquez has tangled, thick, black hair streaked with gray and looks a bit like a pirate. He has continued to write, producing three more novels with South American history as their themes. His latest, *The General in His Labyrinth*, takes Simon Bolívar himself as its hero. Bolívar died at Santa Marta near García Márquez's birthplace, and the novelist has been fascinated with the "Liberator" since boyhood. García Márquez portrays him as an old man sailing down the Magdalena River into exile, bitter with thoughts of his failed dream of a united South America. The Bolívar of the novel is not an idealized, larger-than-life figure; he comes alive with all his faults.

Because of his great success and worldwide fame, García Márquez finds writing has become even more difficult. He must consider his words very carefully, because his fame has brought great responsibility. He has taken on the task of explaining South America's rich culture and tradition, the aspirations and struggles of its people. In his work the "many great and strange things" of the continent have found a voice that speaks to the whole world.

GLOSSARY

Acllausi: "House of the chosen women," the dwelling place of the royal women of the Incas.

Altiplano: A high plateau in the Andean region.

Bandeirantes: "Flag-bearers," adventurers who carried the flag of Portugal into the unknown territory of the New World.

Beata: A religiously devout woman who devoted her life to prayer and good works without formally joining a community of nuns.

Camerera: A woman who was permitted to dress the statue of the Virgin Mary before it was brought out for processions

Caudillo: "Strong man." The term for the local and national dictators who ruled regions and sometimes entire countries through military force and the power of their personalities.

Cholo: Bolivian term for a mestizo.

Chôro: A type of Brazilian popular song. Heitor Villa-Lobos used the name for some of his musical compositions.

Conquistador: "Conquerer" in Spanish, it was the name for the Spanish soldiers who first came to the New World in search of wealth and glory.

Criollo: A person of Spanish or other European ancestry born in America. Feminine: **criolla**.

Descamisados: The "shirtless ones," working-class Argentines who were among Juan D. Perón's greatest supporters.

Estanciero: The owner of a ranch, or *estancia*.

Federales: Argentines who favored a weak centralized government, with power in the hands of local leaders.

Gaucho: A cowboy who worked on the pampas of South America.

Ilanero: Horseman of the huge, swampy grassland of northern South America.

Mantilla: A Spanish woman's long lace scarf worn over the head.

Mazorca: The domestic spy organization of the Argentine caudillo Juan Manuel de Rosas.

Mestizo: A person of mixed Spanish and Native American ancestry. Feminine: **mestiza**.

Pampas: The grassy plains of southeastern South America.

Pardo: A person of mixed race, usually European and African. In Spanish, the word literally means "brown."

Peninsulare: A New World colonist born in Spain, as distinguished from a criollo. See **criollo**.

Quinto: The one-fifth share of all the profits from the Brazilian mines that was sent to the king of Portugal.

Tapada: A woman of colonial Lima who hid her face behind her shawl so that she could flirt with men without revealing her identity.

Unitarios: Argentines who favored a strong centralized government.

BIBLIOGRAPHY

Appleby, David P., *Heitor Villa-Lobos: A Bio-bibliography*. New York: Greenwood Press, 1988.

Arciniegas, Germán, ed., *The Green Continent: A Comprehensive View of Latin America by Its Leading Writers*. New York: Knopf, 1944.

Arnold, Caroline, *Pelé The King of Soccer*, New York: Franklin Watts, 1992.

Cameron, Ian, *Kingdom of the Sun Gods: A History of the Andes and Their People*. New York: Facts on File, 1990.

Castedo, Leopoldo, *The Cuzco Circle*. New York: The Center for Inter-American Relations, 1976.

Chasteen, John Charles, "Maria Antonia Muniz: Frontier Matriarch," from Ewell, Judith, and Beezley, William L., eds, *The Human Tradition in Latin America: The 19th Century*. Wilmington, DE: SR Books, 1989.

Del Par, Helen, ed., *Encyclopedia of Latin America*. New York: McGraw-Hill, 1974.

Downes, Olin, "Heitor Villa-Lobos," New York City Center of Music and Drama program, quoted from *The New York Times*, 12/17/1944.

Gheerbrant, Alain, *The Amazon, Past, Present, and Future*. New York: Abrams, 1992.

Haskins, James, *Pelé, A Biography*. Garden City, NY: Doubleday, 1976.

Henderson, James D., and Henderson, Linda Roddy, *Ten Notable Women of Latin America*. Chicago: Nelson-Hall, 1978.

Herring, Hubert, *A History of Latin America from the Beginnings to the Present*. New York: Knopf, 1961.

Hewlett, John, *Like Moonlight on Snow*. New York: Robert M. McBride, 1947.

Hopkins, Jack W., *Latin America: Perspectives on a Region*. New York: Holmes and Meier, 1987.

Hughes, Langston, translator, *Selected Poems of Gabriela Mistral*. Bloomington, IN: Indiana University Press, 1966.

Keen, Benjamin, and Wasserman, Mark, *A History of Latin America*, 3rd ed. Boston: Houghton Mifflin, 1988.

Mann, Graciela, *The Twelve Prophets of Aleijadinho*. Austin: University of Texas Press, 1967.

Marcus, Joe, *The World of Pelé*. New York: Mason/Charter, 1976.

Martín, Luis, *Daughters of the Conquistadors*. Albuquerque: University of New Mexico Pess, 1983.

Minta, Stephen, *García Márquez, Writer of Colombia*. New York: Harper & Row, 1987.

Onís, Harriet, ed., *The Golden Land: An Anthology of Latin American Folklore in Literature*. New York: Knopf, 1948.

Plenn, Abel, *The Southern Americas: A New Chronicle*. New York: Creative Age Press, 1948.

Robertson, William Spence, *Rise of the Spanish-American Republics as Told in the Lives of Their Liberators*. New York: Free Press, 1965.

Schurz, William Lytle, *This New World: The Civilization of Latin America*. New York: Dutton, 1964.

Skidmore, Thomas E., and Smith, Peter H., *Modern Latin America*. New York: Oxford University Press, 1984.

Smitly, Carleton Sprague, "Villa-Lobos," *Americas*, 11/1950, from typescript in Lincoln Center Library, New York City.

De La Vega, Garcilaso, *The Royal Commentaries of the Incas*, trans. Maria Jolas. New York: Avon Books, 1971.

Wohl, Gary, and Ruibal, Carmen Cadilla, *Hispanic Personalities: Celebrities of the Spanish-Speaking World*. New York: Regents Publishing Company, 1978.

Worcester, Donald, *Makers of Latin America*. New York: Dutton, 1966.

SOURCES

Introduction: El Dorado
page 5: "I said Mass..." Plenn, Abel, The Southern Americas, p. 71.
page 6: "In spite of..." Onís, Harriet, The Golden Land, pp. 14-15.
page 6: "many great and strange..." Schurz, William Lytle, This New World, p. vi.

Chapter 1: Garcilaso de la Vega
page 8: "The Spanish cavalrymen..." De La Vega, Garcilaso, The Royal Commentaries of the Incas, p. 401.
page 11: "Every week..." Schurz, op. cit, p. 42.
pages 11-12: "You should..." Cameron, Ian, Kingdom of the Sun Gods, p. 56.
page 12: "All of these bodies..." Schurz, op. cit., p. xxvii.
page 13: "I came back..." Ibid., p. xxvii.

Chapter 2: Rose of Lima
page 16: "Because they say..." Arciniegas, Germán, ed., The Green Continent, p. 189.
page 17: "When I moved..." Ibid., p. 190.
page 17: "Come, little nightingale..." Ibid., p. 191.

Chapter 3: Antônio Francisco Lisboa
page 25: "so sickly that..." Del Par, Helen, ed., Encyclopedia of Latin America, p. 332.

Chapter 4: Simón Bolívar and José de San Martín
page 26: "To the two greatest men..." Herring, Hubert, A History of Latin America From the Beginnings to the Present, p. 282.
page 28: "You have molded my heart..." Ibid., p. 261.
page 30: "A people that loves freedom..." Wohl, Gary, and Ruibal, Carmen Cadilla, Hispanic Personalities, p. 26.
page 31: "In 1811, I was serving..." Robertson, William Spence, Rise of the Spanish American Republics, p. 176.
page 33: "I do not seek military glory..." Skidmore, Thomas E., and Smith, Peter H., Modern Latin America, p. 35.
pages 33-34: "Believe me..." Robertson, op. cit., p. 244.
page 34: "America is ungovernable..." Skidmore, op. cit., p. 36.

Chapter 5: Maria Antônia Muniz
page 39: "'Twas in the village..." Chasteen, John Charles, "Maria Antônia Muniz: Frontier Matriarch," p. 60.
page 39: "If Brazil demands..." Herring, Hubert, op. cit., p. 291.

Chapter 6: Domingo Faustino Sarmiento
page 43: "primitive barbarity..." Onís, Harriet, op. cit., p.127.

page 44: "Some object..." Ibid., p. 127.
page 44: "I was taken..." Herring, Hubert, op. cit., p 651.
page 46: "Never perhaps has the sun..." Ibid., p. 653.
page 48: "If I do not advance..." Ibid., p. 654.

Chapter 7: Simón I. Patiño
Quotations in this chapter from Hewlett, John, Like Moonlight on Snow, pp. 84, 87,165–66.

Chapter 8: Gabriela Mistral
page 58: "O, River Elqui..." Hughes, Langston, translator, Selected Poems of Gabriela Mistral, p. 111.
page 58: "I was happy until..." Henderson James D. and Henderson, Linda Roddy, Ten Notable Women of Latin America, p. 172.
page 58: "I am one of those..." Ibid., p. 173.
page 59: "A son, a son..." Hughes, Langston, op. cit., p. 61.
page 60: "The blood red rose..." Ibid., p. 72.

Chapter 9: Heitor Villa-Lobos
page 66: "Aha! It isn't here..." Downes, Olin, New York City Center of Music and Drama program, p. 25.
page 67: "This work represents..." Smitly, Carleton Sprague, "Villa-Lobos," p. 6.
page 67: "I can accomplish..." Downes, Olin, op. cit. p. 27.

Chapter 10: Evita Perón
page 71: "I will be somebody..." Worcester, Donald, Makers of Latin America, p. 166.
page 72: "Well, what do you expect..." Henderson, op. cit., p. 200.
page 75: "I have wanted..." Ibid., p. 21.

Chapter 11: Pelé
page 78: "I have never seen..." Marcus, Joe, The World of Pelé, pp. 31-32.
page 78: "Look at his legs..." Haskins, James, Pelé, p. 39.
page 79: "The harder I tried..." Marcus, Joe, op. cit., p. 10.
page 81: "I feel the divine gift..." Haskins, James, op. cit., p. 99.
page 81: "For me there will be no more..." Arnold, Caroline, Pelé the King of Soccer, p. 32.
page 82: "Brazil is a very rich country..." Ibid., p. 56.

Chapter 12: Gabriel García Márquez
pages 83-84: "Many years later..." Márquez, Gabriel García, One Hundred Years of Solitude, pp. 11-26.
page 85: "In that house..." Minta, Stephen, García Márquez, p. 34.
page 86: "It's possible..." Ibid., p. 37.
page 86: "I arrived from..." Ibid., pp. 38-39.
page 87: "For three years..." Ibid., p. 147.

INDEX

Acosta, Miguel, 15
Amaro da Silveira family, 35, 38-41
Amaro da Silveira, Domingos, 40
Amaro da Silveira, Manuel, 35, 38, 40
Amazon River, 5, 6
Andes Mountains, 4, 7, 30, 32, 43, 45, 49
Apac, 49
Aracataca, Colombia, 85
Atahualpa, 8, 10
Bello, Andres, 28
Bogotá, Colombia, 86
Bolívar, Simón, 26-31, 33-34, 89
Bonaparte, Napoleon, 28, 29, 31, 39
Buenos Aires, Argentina, 31, 45, 47, 69, 71, 72
Caracas, Venezuela, 28, 29, 30
Carvajal, Gaspar de, 5
Chaco War, 55
Ciudad Bolívar, Venezuela, 30
Cochabamba, Bolivia, 49, 53, 54
conquistadors, 4, 5
Cuzco, Peru, 7, 8, 10, 12, 13
Duarte, María Eva, *See* Perón, Evita
El Dorado, 4
"El Inca," *See* Vega, Garcilaso de la
Franklin, Benjamin, 44
Godoy, Lucila, *See* Mistral, Gabriela
Guayaquil, Ecuador, 26, 28
Huayna Capac, 8, 12

Inca Empire, 4, 8, 10, 11-12
Jefferson, Thomas, 24
Jesuits, 23
Lake Titicaca, 12
LaMarque, Libertad, 69
Lima, Peru, 15, 16, 33
Lisboa, Antônio Francisco, 20-25
Lisboa, Manuel Francisco de, 21, 22
Mann, Horace, 47, 48
Márquez, Gabriel García, 83-89
Mauricio, 24, 25
Minas Gerais, 22, 24, 78
Mistral, Gabriela, 57-62
Muniz, Maria Antônia, 35-41
Napo River, 5
Nascimento, Edson Arantes do, *See* Pelé
Nobel Prize for Literature, 62, 89
Nusta Chimpu Ocllo, 10
O'Higgins, Bernardo, 32, 33
Orellana, Francisco de 5, 6
Ouro Prêto, Brazil, 21, 22, 24
Patiño, Simón I., 49-55
Patiño, Albina Rodríguez, 51, 52, 53, 54
Pedro I, Emperor of Brazil, 39
Pelé, 77-82
Perón, Evita, 69-75
Perón, Isabelita, 75
Perón, Juan D., 69, 71-75
Pizarro, Francisco, 4, 7, 8, 10
Pizarro, Gonzalo, 4, 5, 7
Punta Arenas, Chile, 59
Quesada, Jiménez de, 4, 86

Quiroga, Facundo, 43-44, 45, 46
Quito, Ecuador, 4, 5, 7
Rímac River, 15
Rio de Janeiro, Brazil, 39, 41, 47, 63, 65, 66, 68, 81
Rio Grande do Sul, 37, 41
Rodríguez, Simón, 28
Rosas, Juan Manuel de, 45, 46, 74
Rosas, Maria de la Encarnación, 45, 74
Rose of Lima, Saint, 14-19
Rubinstein, Arthur, 66, 67
San Martín, José de, 26, 31-34, 44
Sâo Paulo, Brazil, 79
Sarmiento, Domingo Faustino, 43-48
Silva Xavier, Joaquim Jose da ("Tiradentes"), 24, 25
Sucre, Antônio José, 34
Ureta, Romelio, 58, 59
Valparaiso, Chile, 45
Vargas, Getúlio, 67, 79
Vega, Garcilaso de la, 7-13
Vega, Sebastian de la, 10
Villa-Lobos, Heitor, 63-68
Violencia, La, 87
War of a Thousand Days, 86, 87
World Cup, 77, 80, 81, 82